samurai girl The Book of the Wind

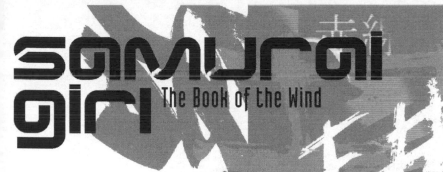

samurai
girl
The Book of the Wind

忍者の訓練

SIMON AND SCHUSTER

SIMON AND SCHUSTER

First published in Great Britain in 2005 by Simon & Schuster
A CBS Company
1st Floor, 222 Gray's Inn Road, London WC1X 8HB

Originally published in 2004 by Simon Pulse, an imprint
of Simon & Schuster Children's Division. New York

Produced by 17th Street Productions, Inc.
A division of Daniel Weiss Associates, Inc.
33 West 17th Street, New York, NY 10011

Text copyright © 2004 by 17th Street Productions, an Alloy company.
Cover illustration copyright © 2004 chenna@www.synergyart.co.uk

A CIP catalogue record for this book is
available from the British Library

ISBN 978 0 689 861277

1 3 5 7 9 10 8 6 4 2

Printed and bound by CPI Group (UK) Ltd, Croydon, CR0 4YY

From the pages of *Bubble World*, a club life 'zine from southern California

The members of Japanese drum-'n'-bass outfit Funkitout have a lot of mystery surrounding them. There are rumours that they are members of the yakuza, stunt doubles in street-fighting films, video game champions, or maybe club kids who spend too much time in Shibuya during the day, hoping to make a cameo appearance in big-budget MTV video shoots. (Rumour has it that when Mariah Carey came over to shoot one of her latest videos, Yukio, Funkitout's lead singer, begged her to listen to a couple of the band's tracks, but Yukio staunchly denies it, saying he never listens to Mariah Carey, and besides, he wasn't even in Shibuya the day her video was filmed.) No one knows for sure what they're all about (they're more secretive and strange than Jack and Meg White of The White Stripes), and even more speculation has arisen with their underground club hit that's been growing in popularity, "Heaven's Gone." The song tells about a girl who mysteriously disappeared from a rich and powerful family and is supposedly from the point of view of her ex-fiancé. But who is this Heaven girl of the song? Is she really, as some have postulated, Heaven Kogo, missing princess of the Kogo empire? Does Funkitout know who she is, or are they just making a social commentary? And why bring that sort of message to the drum-'n'-bass world? We asked some kids at Club Dragonfly in Los Angeles what they think:

Girl with multicoloured dreadlocks, a pacifier on a string around her neck: "I think this Heaven chick is some ex-girlfriend who realized that Yukio was messing with about six other girls. If you notice in the song it goes, 'Got my girls in a huddle on the club couch,' and then it says later, 'Heaven says it's over sportin' keys to my Rover.' So it's obvious this Heaven girl wised up and got outta there. Boys don't know how good they got it when they got a solid girl by their side."

Japanese boy in a brightly coloured anime soccer shirt: "My cousin lives in Japan and IM'ed me to say that this Heaven girl is actually a real person. The daughter of some dude named Konishi. She sounds like a total ice queen. The song is awesome. Yukio's probably psyched she's gone."

American boy, hat on tilt à la Nelly, Band-Aid under his left eye: "Dude, as long as the beat's strong, that's all I'm trippin' on. But as long as you're askin', this Heaven chick was probably some girl who got sick of waiting around for a guy to realize he was mad crazy for her. So she took off and did her own thing. But he realized, yo. It was like that absence makes the heart grow fonder thing. I'm goin' through the same thing with this ex-girlfriend of mine. I made a colossal mistake. But don't put that in print."

The flames surrounded us.

I shivered inside my coat and watched as my house – well, the house I'd been living in for the past month or so – spat and hissed in a mountain of fire and smoke. Fire engines rushed to the scene. Eight men tumbled out of the truck and started rolling the hose towards a fire hydrant.

"Everyone get back!" one of them yelled.

Hiro pulled on my arm. "We have to move back, Heaven," he said.

I felt cemented to the ground. Cheryl, my housemate, was trapped inside.

Who set this fire?

Marcus?

I had left him back at the subway station. Cheryl had come home by herself in a cab. The driver had promised to walk her to the door. Hiro and I were only minutes behind her in another cab.

Meaning . . . if I hadn't gone back to the club to get my bag . . . I would've been inside the house, too. The heat started to affect my skin. The smoke began to burn my eyes. I felt light-headed and woozy. My whole body ached.

"Come on," Hiro said again. "We've got to get out of here."

I stared up at my bedroom window and thought, fleetingly, of my sad assortment of personal belongings trapped inside. The jeans and trainers I bought when I first got to L.A. My crumpled-up photograph of my brother, Ohiko, which I carried with me in my shiro-maku wedding kimono. Various clothes belonging to Hiro. I didn't have much – I hadn't saved enough money yet to really have many material possessions. But still, everything that was mine since I'd come to L.A. was turning to ash and fluttering away.

My eyes filled with tears.

"Heaven, we've got to move," Hiro said, tugging on my arm. "Come on."

A large piece of the roof cracked and fell mere inches from us. Hiro jumped back, but I stood and stared. The flames leapt and danced.

"You're acting foolish!" Hiro said, pulling on my sleeve.

"Wait," I said softly. I saw my little bedroom window, behind the branches of the big cedar tree. Flames danced around the window frame. Was it possible that maybe

Cheryl hadn't come home? Perhaps she'd gone somewhere else . . . like to the diner or maybe to the hospital to get her ankle looked at . . .

Hiro dragged me under a tree. "You're pale," he said, moving his face close to mine. "Come on. We have to get a cab and get out of this neighbourhood." He pulled at me. "Heaven . . . you've been so strong so far."

It was true – I *had* been completely strong up until this moment. I had just defended Cheryl from Marcus, who was more terrifying than I'd ever imagined. I'd narrowly avoided death, meeting a subway car head-on. Marcus had dragged Cheryl away from the club knowing I'd follow them. He *knew* that I'd been suspicious of him from the word go. And he *knew* I'd defend Cheryl. He'd lured me down to that subway station. It had all been a plot to corner me.

And the fire. It was most likely for me as well.

I breathed in and out, trying to get a grip. The firemen worked on, spraying parts of the house to stop the flames. I stepped out from under the tree and moved towards the burning piece of roof again.

"Who wants me dead so badly?" I said aloud. Could it be the Yukemuras?

But it didn't make sense. The Yukemuras, dangerous as they were, didn't want me dead. Yoji, the head of the Yukemura clan, needed me to marry Teddy for the agreed-upon "booty". They had to have me alive. At least for a little while longer.

"Surround and drown!" one of the firemen bellowed. "The inside's collapsing!"

No. It had to be someone else.

I crept up a little closer. My mind circled back to one person. *Mieko.*

Mieko, my stepmother. I'd called her a couple of days ago. I needed to see how my father was doing – he'd been in a coma for almost a month. And when I heard her familiar voice come on the line, she sounded friendly – loving, almost.

And believe me, Mieko isn't the friendly type.

We didn't talk about our family. Instead Mieko grilled me about what I was doing. What was my address? she asked again and again.

"It looks like we've got a class B here," one of the firemen shouted into his radio. "Send us some backup."

Marcus had mentioned Mieko. In the subway station he'd said, "Your mother says hello."

How did Mieko know Marcus?

More voices rang out. "Check the window! Is anyone still in there?"

Bricks crashed to the ground.

But I *hadn't* given her my address. I'd got off the phone before I gave away any important information.

But if she knew Marcus . . . who was kind of dating Cheryl . . . who lived with me . . .

My head spun. *Why* did Mieko know *Marcus*?

I stared up at the burning house and my hands curled into fists. The heat made my eyes water. The photo of Ohiko up there was burning up, right now, possibly because of Mieko or Marcus. Its sides were at that very moment curling and blackening. The fire would eat away Ohiko's face.

All at once, before I knew what I was doing, I ran to the house. The firemen had hosed down the front yard, and the grass squished under my feet. One of the men grabbed my arm with his thick glove as I rushed past.

"What are you *doing*?" he asked.

I shook free of his grip. I heard Hiro's screams from behind me. The smoke was overpowering, but I pushed my way in.

The inside of the house was like nothing I'd ever seen. Orange flames shot from the mantel, the couch, the floor. All of Cheryl's little knick-knacks – and she had a lot of random stuff – were charred and blurred into a huge ball of fire.

I heard noises from upstairs.

"Cheryl?" I screamed. I ran to the stairway, but the whole thing was lit up in flames. All of a sudden a rush of air shot towards me, and I saw fingers of fire dance down the banister.

My God. If Cheryl was up there, she was definitely dead.

I looked around me. I'd never realized how *loud* fire was. The sound of the crackling and the growing flames was *deafening*. And it was surrounding me.

Ohiko's photo was up there. That was the only thing I had left of him. What if I forgot what he looked like? I windmilled my arms right and left, lifting my feet, trying to avoid the flames. A loud crash behind me made me flinch. I wheeled around; the chimney had fallen off the far wall. The flames were devouring it.

Screw it. I had to get out of here. The smoke stung my eyes. I looked down at Cheryl's end table. Her grandmother's necklace, a gold chain with a large antique amethyst stone, was draped over the edge of a small bowl. Nothing was on fire yet.

Before I knew what I was doing, I grabbed it, and rushed out the door. The smoke blinded me.

I shoved the necklace into my pocket. Firemen rushed around me. "Are you all right?" they screamed. Two men picked me up and carried me away from the house.

"Why the hell did you go in there?" one of the firemen yelled. "Are you out of your *mind*?"

I coughed. Hiro ran up to me. "What were you *doing*?" he asked.

I didn't say anything. I felt deadened. My heart beat fast.

"We've got to get out of here," Hiro said. "Fast. This isn't safe for us." I could tell he was pissed. And worried. "Come on, try to stand up."

I stood up, but my knees buckled. The smoke had made me dizzy.

"All right all right, sit down for a minute," Hiro said. "I

don't know why you went back in there – you could have
been killed! The inhalation of smoke alone could have
knocked you out!"

"I'm okay," I said. I didn't want to tell him about Cheryl's
necklace. He'd ask me why I'd taken it. And I didn't know
why myself.

I breathed in and out steadily, trying to remember my
pranayama breath. I could hear the stream of water hitting the side of Cheryl's house. *Get a grip, Heaven,* I told
myself.

I slowly pressed my palms to the ground and lifted
myself up. I felt a little better. Hiro chased down a cab. He
opened the door for me. "Come on, get in," he said. "We're
going to get far away from this."

I fell onto the seat and could smell the smoke on my
clothes. Hiro climbed in, too. The cabby idled, waiting for us
to tell him where to go.

"Where are we going?" I asked. The fire lit up his face.
The orange glow made him look more handsome than ever.
His cheekbones seemed prominent; his eyes were deep-set
and sensual. I even got turned on looking at the curve of his
forearm. On the cab ride over here, I'd got butterflies from
the way he looked at me. Our knees had gently touched.
Hiro had grabbed my hand. Looked carefully and soulfully
into my eyes.

Despite my delirium, chills ran up and down my spine
just thinking about him.

"I don't know where we'll go," he said, looking over his shoulder at the burning house.

"Where to?" the cabby grumbled.

"Wait just a second, please," Hiro said, then turned to me. "Let's go back to my place."

"No," I said. "Your house is an obvious target. What if it's being watched right now? Maybe we should go to a diner or something to sit and figure this out." I fumbled with the strap of my bag. I also didn't want to go to Hiro's because his girlfriend, Karen, might be there. I hadn't faced her since we'd had a huge fight about Hiro in the park a couple of days ago.

"I don't think we should be anywhere well lit right now. Nothing seems safe," Hiro said, looking out the back window. "What about one of the empty warehouses we've done training sessions in? Like the one down on Winston?"

I thought of the abandoned warehouses in downtown L.A. Creepy. When the Yukemuras had kidnapped Karen (a big reason why Karen and I had been on the rocks lately – that and the fact that she wanted me to "stay away from Hiro"), the "exchange" had taken place at a decrepit parking garage somewhere downtown. It was beyond spooky. I had a feeling the Yukemuras frequented areas like that. Vibe was down there, too. I didn't really feel like going back into that mess.

"Nope," I said. "No way."

Great. We'd pretty much determined that I had nowhere left to go. Instantly I was homeless again. "We should just drive out of the city, far, far away," I said, not very sarcastically. I felt completely drained of energy. Hiro had had to deal with this problem twice before – once when I'd showed up on his doorstep, blood spattered and terrified, and then when I'd had to move out due to a random attack right in front of his apartment building on Lily Place. I mean, he had to be getting sick of shuttling me around so that I would always be safe. No wonder he wasn't into me.

"Really, getting out of the city would be the best thing to do," Hiro murmured.

"You kids going anywhere or what?" the cabdriver bellowed. "This smoke is getting to me."

"One moment, please. I'm really sorry," Hiro said.

"Maybe there *is* somewhere I could go that's not in the city," I said softly. But it was such a long shot. I knew Hiro would say it was too dangerous.

"Where?" he asked.

"To see my friend Katie," I said. I couldn't believe I was even telling him my idea. But I felt nervous sitting there in the cab, not moving. "My tutor, remember? She was my best friend in Japan. She moved to Vegas – that's where she's from – after my wedding. I mean, she wasn't *at* my wedding or anything. She moved back a couple of weeks before I got here." I put my finger to my lips. "I wonder if she even knows what happened."

"So you're saying . . . Las Vegas," Hiro said slowly.

"I think that may be best," I said.

"Do you know where Katie lives?"

"Well, no," I said. I'd called information once before to track her down, but there was no listing for her. And I'd left her mother's number in the hotel room on the day of my wedding. "But . . ."

Hiro didn't say anything. I would have loved to see Katie again. But I didn't know where she *lived* in Vegas, or where she worked, or if she was even still there or not.

I pressed on. "I do remember that she said she was moving to Vegas after my wedding to get a job in one of the casinos."

Hiro looked at me incredulously. "Isn't that a strange transition to make? From being an English tutor to working at a casino?"

I shrugged. "I don't know," I said. "Katie . . . she's a risk taker. She came over from the States to tutor me, didn't she? Why not go to Vegas after that?"

"Huh," Hiro said. I frowned.

"Besides," I said. "It's not like I have much going for me here in L.A." This was true: I had no friends. Cheryl was dead. Hiro and I could never be together. And he had a beautiful girlfriend who hated me and wasn't afraid to say it.

Hiro didn't say anything. *Maybe he agrees,* I thought.

"I could take a bus there and look for her," I continued. "The bus would be much safer than a plane – more anonymous. And I have some money on me from working, so I could stay in a hotel while I looked for Katie."

Hiro cleared his throat after a few moments. "I think that might be the best idea," he said slowly.

I nodded. "I think so, too," I said. But inside, my stomach started to gurgle with anxiety.

"Take us to the Greyhound bus station," he told the cabdriver. We zoomed off.

I looked at him. He shrugged. "You're right," he said. "The case you made for going to Las Vegas is a better idea than anything we can come up with in L.A."

"Of course," I said, hiding my shock. "Let's go, then."

I stared out the window as the cab zoomed towards the freeway. Hiro looked out the other window. I longed for the togetherness we'd been feeling on the cab ride to my house (*Hiro touching my hand, Hiro telling me how strong and incredible I was, Hiro denying he was moving in with Karen, Hiro's gorgeous face, his hot body, his delicious skin, his soft hands . . .*)

But he thought I should go to Vegas.

We pulled up to a large lot in front of a squat, dimly lit building. A few buses were idling in the lot. The red, white, and blue Greyhound logo flickered on the top of the building.

"Swanky," I whispered.

Hiro leaned in to the cabdriver. "We're dropping her off," he said. "If you could wait here for a moment for me . . . I'm going back to Echo Park." The cabby nodded.

"You're having the cab *wait*?" I said, my voice breaking

a little. All of this was catching up to me. One minute, we were standing in front of my burning house. Suddenly the next, Hiro was shuttling me off to Las Vegas with barely a goodbye! He was having the cab *wait* for him! Meaning . . . he only wanted to see me off for a minute or two! When did he think a bus was going to show up?

"I don't have any clothes," I blurted, uncertain. "They've all burned up in the fire."

"You can get new ones in Las Vegas," Hiro said. He wiped his palms on his trousers. I glared at him, suddenly angry. It was pitch-dark out. There was no one at the bus station. It was *creepy*. What was his problem? Why was he just leaving me like this, on the curb? What had made his mood change? How could he just drive home and snuggle into his warm bed with Karen at his side while I staggered onto some smelly bus to a city I'd never even seen?

My throat went dry. I didn't want to show Hiro how nervous I was. Instead I let my emotions turn to controlled rage. *Fine. So he thinks I should get out of town. Well, then, I'll go. Sayonara.*

I walked up to the counter as chill as possible and checked the timetable. A bus for Las Vegas would be leaving in an hour. I glanced behind the ticket window, but it was dark and empty. I turned to Hiro, but he was standing with his back to me, facing the car. I breathed out, frustrated, and walked as calmly as I could over to the Greyhound To-Go machine console. I shoved money in, and out popped a ticket. I examined it, trying to figure out what it said under the dim lights.

"The bus is in an hour," I said, walking back to him. Hiro turned. The cab lights lit up his face, and my heart flipped over.

"So," I said in an authoritarian voice. I wanted to be fully in Independent Heaven mode when I said goodbye to Hiro. "What about training? If I find Katie and everything – I mean, *when* I find Katie – I'm going to want to keep up my training. Should I check in with you every once in a while? Are you going to want to give me drills or something?"

Hiro shook his head slightly and stepped closer to me. He put his hands softly on my shoulders. Tingles instantly rushed through me. "Listen," he said. "This is very important. You have to listen to me carefully. When I get back into this cab and leave you, I want you to forget all about me."

I breathed in sharply.

"I want you to forge your way ahead, Heaven. Make your own life. Become your own rock. Train according to your own needs. Find your training within yourself." He spoke slowly and evenly, not quite looking into my eyes but instead at a faraway place, past the bus station.

I stared at him, completely dumbstruck. "Say *what*?" I sputtered finally.

He stood there, arms crossed, a look of total serenity on his face. I mean, Hiro always had a pretty deadpan expression on his face *anyway*, but I expected him to crack up soon.

He shook his head. "I'm not joking. It's your mission. This is very serious."

I felt a movement behind me and flinched. But it was only the stationmaster, unlocking his booth. He nodded at me. "You're here a little early, aren't you?" he asked. I looked back at Hiro. I had an hour to kill. They could find me here. The people looking for me. The people who set fire to that house. The Yukemuras. So many people.

He didn't meet my gaze. "I have to go," he said.

"But . . . ," I squeaked. "The bus . . . is in . . . an hour!" *Don't lose it,* I told myself. *Keep it together.* Instead I blurted, "Does this mean you don't want . . . me . . . around?"

Hiro looked out at the cab. He purposefully wasn't looking in my direction. What was his *deal*?

"It's not that, Heaven. My feelings for you are . . . very strong . . . You don't understand . . . but . . ." He put his head down. He bit his lip, turned away. "This is what we have to do." His voice sounded muffled, strange.

"What are you *talking* about?" I said. I knew I sounded desperate. "What do you mean your feelings are strong? Why is this what you have to do? I don't get it!"

"I . . . I can't explain it now," Hiro said. "Forget me. Please. You have to. Now go wait for your bus." He pointed at a bench. I tried to speak, but no words came out.

The cabdriver peered out disintrestedly at Hiro. "You getting in or what?" he growled.

"Goodbye," Hiro said to me, still avoiding my eyes. And then, without even a touch – much less a kiss – he turned and got inside the waiting cab.

"Goodbye," I said softly. I watched him get in the cab and instruct the driver to take him back to Echo Park. I chewed the edge of my lip, then turned away as the cab pulled out of the lot. I didn't want to look at him.

I have to drop her off and leave. This is not an easy decision, obviously. I cannot wait with her.

But this is all part of the flow of things. This is necessary.

The cab drives me around the corner, and I stop him. "Let me off here," I say. I get out and stand in the bushes, watching her from a distance. She sits next to the stationmaster, on the bench. She looks terrified. Confused.

I've asked her to embark on a very serious journey.

Have I just made a big mistake?

After a long time the bus pulls up. She lifts herself off the bench and climbs aboard. She is getting on. She is going.

I think of the people I know of in Las Vegas. Not good people. People that I have wanted to get away from. But they will always be there. Will they find her? Will she be able to take care of herself on her own?

What is she feeling? What if she fails in her mission?

I have to remain calm. There is a lesson in every journey that we take – I know this for myself. But I am still learning. I breathe deeply. L.A. is just beginning to wake up.

She's stronger than I originally thought. She's stronger than I am, in many ways.

This is the first day without Heaven here.

I think of the fable that my mother once told me. Once upon a time, a young man named Mikeran was walking home after working in the fields. As he passed by the shore of a lake, he spotted something hanging from a tree. He wondered what it was – it looked like a robe.

But it was not like any robe he had seen before. It shone like a bright star. Mikeran was delighted with his find. I must have it, he thought. He took the robe down, folded it, and put it in his basket. He was about to walk away when someone called out to him. "Did someone call me?" he asked, looking around. "Who is there?"

"I did." Out of the grass by the lake stepped the most beautiful young woman Mikeran had ever seen. "My name is Tanabata. Please give me back my celestial robe," she said.

Mikeran was confused.

The woman continued. "Without it, I cannot return to my home in heaven." She was nearly ready to cry. "I don't belong on earth. I only came here to bathe in this lovely lake. I beg you, give me back my robe!"

"I don't know what you're talking about," he lied. "I haven't seen any robe."

Rather than allow her to return to her heavenly home, Mikeran forced Tanabata to live in his house with him. Eventually the two grew to love each other. Happy as she was with her earthly life, however, Tanabata longed for her true home.

Then one day when Mikeran was out working in the fields, Tanabata noticed that a bird was pecking at something between the roof beams. To her horror, the bird pulled out a piece of beautiful, glittering cloth.

"My robe!" Tanabata cried. Mikeran had known about it all along and was keeping it from her.

That evening Mikeran returned from the fields to find his wife waiting outside in her celestial garment. He drew in his breath.

Tanabata nodded sadly, lifted her hands towards heaven, and began to rise into the air. As she rose, she looked down at her husband and said, "Mikeran . . . if you really love me, weave a thousand pairs of straw sandals and bury them beneath the bamboo. If you do, we can meet again."

Mikeran watched helplessly as Tanabata rose higher and higher in the sky until all he could see was the shining robe.

Mikeran was not able to weave that many sandals in his lifetime. They say these two lovers only meet one day out of the year – on the seventh day of the seventh month. In the sky they are called Altair and Vega. I'm not sure why I'm reminded of this just now. Maybe because of my own feelings of frustration. I wanted to tell Heaven how I felt. I know she wanted me to explain it to her.

But it was not the right time.

I try not to think of this.

I catch the bus for the long ride home. Finally I come to my lighted window. Karen must be up early. I see her there, looking out. She sees me but does not wave. I look away. What is wrong with me lately? I'm feeling a pull, somehow, towards someone else. Something else. I look back at Karen. She stands before the window, luminous and beautiful, peering out at nothing. I'm wondering if my decision was the right one.

I look away again. I can't deny it. I want it to be some-one else up there in that window, lying in my bed, waiting for me to come home. Wondering where I've been. Waiting to start the day with me.

Hiro

2

They announced my bus. I walked towards it like a zombie and climbed aboard. There were only three other people – old ladies who'd woken up at 4 a.m., it seemed – who boarded with me. I took a seat, careful to avoid a huge wad of gum stuck between the chair and the window.

Mission, my ass.

Hiro wanted to get rid of me.

That had to be it. He wanted to get rid of me.

But what had he been trying to say? *My feelings for you are very strong, but . . .*

But *what*?

Then the bus began to fill.

"I can't wait," one of the women sitting next to me said, craning her neck to see out the front window. "Vegas." She smiled. "You ever been to Vegas before?"

"No," I said tentatively. The last thing I wanted right now was to talk to some old woman who had a gambling problem.

"You'll love it," she said.

Mission. Ha. I could hear Hiro's voice: "This mission is not about me, Heaven. This mission is about *Samurai Girl*."

"Lies," I said quietly. Who was Samurai Girl, anyway? I turned uncomfortably and something stabbed my hip. Cheryl's necklace. I pulled it out and examined it. It was really gorgeous. Purple, sort of translucent. A heavy stone. Not my style, really, but still really fancy and interesting.

"That's a nice necklace," the same old lady said. "Are you going to use that for gambling?"

"Excuse me?" I asked tiredly.

"You know, pawn it," she said. Her teeth were yellow.

"Um, no," I said. But maybe I could use it if I ran out of money. I shoved it back in my pocket.

We drove and drove. I fell asleep for a couple of minutes, shell-shocked. And then, all of a sudden, we rolled into the heart of Vegas. The bus coughed and wheezed up what definitely must be called "the Strip".

I pressed my nose to the window. What *was* this place? I mean, I knew something about Vegas from movies and stuff. But this was . . . this was . . . dirty and gritty and sort of gross. It was about 10 a.m. The sun was hot and oppressive. We rumbled by the casinos. They were huge and lit by strange, desert light. They looked tired. We whooshed by a gigantic Statue of Liberty that looked . . . I don't know . . .

like it was made out of papier-mâché. The Eiffel Tower danced into view. The next casino was full of Roman columns and fountains. A Ferris wheel peeked out from behind another row of casinos.

The heat clung to my arms and legs. My hair stuck to the back of my neck. I smelled like a bonfire. My fingernails were dirty. Since it was pretty early in the morning, the only people roaming around were harmless-looking families with back packs. But Vegas seemed . . . grimy and old. I'd expected neon, shiny stuff, opulence, style, diamonds, money . . .

"It doesn't get good until it gets dark," my bus mate said. I nodded. Hopefully she was right.

Katie. Was she really here? I tried to remember one of my last conversations with her. Immediately one came to mind: it was right after I got engaged, and right before she spoke out in opposition to my marrying Teddy Yukemura.

Katie had brought over a pile of fun prom magazines and we were looking through them for prom dresses. I obviously wouldn't be wearing an American sort of wedding dress for my ceremony – my father had made it clear I was to wear a tsuno kakushi wedding hood and a "fan of happiness" in my obi belt, along with my very un-American wedding kimono – but it was fun to look at all the tulle and the beads and the high-heeled pointy shoes and the fun hair all the girls wore when going off to their fairy-tale school dances with the date of their dreams. We were marking the styles that we liked the best.

"Yatsumi for some reason likes dresses and shirts with no backs, like halters," Katie said absentmindedly.

"How do you know *that*?" I asked her. Yatsumi was a gardener who worked on our grounds from time to time. He was flat-out *gorgeous*. He looked like Keanu Reeves: rugged, rough, a little wild. I'd watched *The Matrix* a million times and dreamed of Yatsumi instead of Keanu. I'd talked about my crush on him a couple of times to Katie; of course, nothing could come of it because before I was engaged, I wasn't allowed to date. And I doubted that Yatsumi would've been my father's choice of date for me anyway, Teddy or no.

Katie gave me a look that was full of guilty surprise. "Oh . . . um, well . . ." And then she grabbed my hands. "I was supposed to keep it a secret, but I went on a couple of dates with him."

"Really?" I asked. "But—"

"Yeah," she said. "He took me to a couple of cafés and a couple of bars, and he even took me to see *How to Lose a Guy in 10 Days* – even though it's such a girlie movie!"

I frowned and looked at the floor.

"It's just for fun, though," Katie said. "We'll see where it goes. I mean, I may want to go to the States after you're married, so I can't take it too seriously."

"Wow, I'm jealous," I said, trying to be light and kidding. "You get to have so much fun . . . You'll have a blast once you're outta this household."

"Yeah, well . . . ," Katie said. "I don't really have a plan of where I'm gonna go. But I do have a cousin who has connections at a casino in Las Vegas. I can make awesome money there. So that might be fun for a while."

Working at a casino in Vegas sounded like a hell of a lot more fun than marrying Teddy Yukemura. *Anything* sounded more fun – mopping the floor, dancing naked, being one of those people who dresses up as a piece of fruit or a cartoon character and hands out flyers on the street. God, Katie could have this fun life – dates with gorgeous guys, adventures in Vegas, *freedom*, and I was under lock and key. The whole conversation had really bummed me out. I'd forgotten about it until now. But recalling our talk made me realize that Katie had *definitely* mentioned that she *might* be going to Vegas. Although if she'd mentioned a specific casino, it had gone right out of my head.

Damn.

The bus stopped and we trooped off. We were right in front of the Flamingo casino. I could see palm trees peeking out from behind its creamy facade. I shaded my eyes from the sun. The people meandering down the Strip were the same sort of American tourists who came to Tokyo and gaped and pointed. But like the old lady said, maybe it would get better at night.

I hadn't slept well on the bus, so I could barely keep my eyes open as I wagged my head right and left, peering at one side of the Strip, then gazing, squinty eyed, at the other. I wandered into the Flamingo and immediately sank into one of the large leather sofas in the lobby.

Hiro and I stood together in front of his house. Except it looked more like the house that, until quite recently, I'd lived in with my family in Japan. Hiro held my hand. He turned to face me. "Wasn't it beautiful?" he asked.

"Wasn't what beautiful?" I said.

"The ceremony," Hiro said, turning to me, looking quite shocked. I noticed he was wearing a very formal charcoal grey suit and a well-knotted, perfectly matching tie. I looked down at my own outfit and saw that I was wearing a very high collared Chinese-style cheongsam dress. In a pure ivory white. I'd never owned such a dress. I'd never even wanted one, although I remembered liking the chartreuse one that Nicole Kidman had worn to the Oscars. But anyway. In my hands I carried a bouquet of flowers.

"What ceremony?" I asked. Hiro looked at me, still astounded. He gestured at my finger.

"Look," he said. "We are married now."

I looked down. A diamond ring was on my finger. I gasped. It was huge. Bigger than the one Ben gave J.Lo. "What?" I said. "But I thought you wanted me to forget you . . ."

Just then a huge, long black car parked in the driveway revved its engine. And just then the door opened – a door that was identical to my front door in Tokyo – and out

28

stepped Mieko, in a bloodred dress cut similarly to mine. She stood on the porch for a moment or two, looking around. She was holding something – blankets? Big grey blankets? – in her arms. Suddenly she looked at Hiro and me and broke into hysterical laughter.

"What is her problem?" I asked. Hiro didn't answer. "What's going on here, anyway?"

Mieko continued to laugh. "My little Heaven," she said.

Then I noticed what she was holding: several of my father's suit jackets and trousers. I recognized the label on the inside of them – sometimes I would watch as one of our maids, Yumiko, pressed his stuff, and the labels, with fancy names like Gucci and Dolce & Gabbana, always caught my eye. Beyond that, I didn't know how I knew – but they were definitely my father's suits.

"What's she doing with those?" I asked. Mieko just kept on laughing. "Why is she taking his suits out of the house?"

Hiro looked at me. His shoulders fell forward. "I don't know, but I will protect you now. Not your father." He looked at me, bent forward to kiss me. I closed my eyes. But the kiss never came. I opened my eyes, and he was gone.

Mieko kept laughing. The big car in the driveway pulled back, then drove away. Hiro was inside.

Someone poked me. "Miss," said a sharp voice. "*Miss.*"

I opened my eyes. What had I been *dreaming* about? I jumped. Where was my bag? I felt for it. It was at my feet. A

29

woman in a hotel uniform glared at me. What day was it? Why wasn't I in my bed at Cheryl's house? Then I remembered. Cheryl's house was a pile of ashes by now. I was in . . .

Las Vegas.

My eyes sprang open even wider.

The woman tapped her foot. "I've let you sleep here long enough. You're going to have to go back to your room."

I looked at her, confused. Then I realized that she thought I was a guest. I looked at my watch. I'd slept for nearly two hours.

"Sorry," I said. The woman rolled her eyes and turned angrily back to the desk.

I got out of there. The open air felt great. The Strip was still kinda seedy, but it seemed a little more crowded now.

I walked to Caesars. It looked pretty swanky. I wondered if Katie was inside. I stopped, confused about to where to go. The pulsating lights seemed to hold me hostage; all of a sudden I couldn't move. People flooded around me. I held my bag tight to my chest.

"You looking for someone?" a voice asked.

I wheeled around and saw a woman in the tiniest sparkly bikini top. I wondered how she wasn't falling out of it. She looked like something out of *Moulin Rouge* with all the make-up she was wearing.

"Yes," I said.

The woman shifted her weight to one hip. Her stiletto heels sparkled. Her whole face sparkled, too – she'd put a ton of glittery blush on. I was certain she was wearing false eyelashes.

"Yes," I said again. "Katie . . . Katie Riley? She works here . . . somewhere . . ." I knew I sounded like a major idiot. It was like those people who said to you, "You're Japanese? I knew a Japanese guy named Kujo or Yoji or Masashi a couple of years ago. You know him?"

The woman looked back and forth and gestured to a side street. I could see more casinos glowing in the distance. "They've got a Katie in the Rio," she said, winking. "She works the tables. Ya wanna see the show? It's my break, and I'm bored."

Could I really have got it right on the first try? Come on. I wasn't that naive. But before I could answer, the woman grabbed me by the arm and started dragging me down the street. Ahead I could see a splashy casino called the Rio.

"You'll love the show," the woman chattered on. I don't know how she could walk in those heels, but she was managing fine. She looked me up and down. "You just get into town?"

"Yeah," I said softly.

"What's with your eye? Did someone hit you?"

Marcus had socked me last night. I touched my eye and quickly shut it. "Not exactly," I said.

"I got some make-up for that . . . ," she said. I shook my head. "Where's the rest of your luggage?"

"Well . . . ," I started. I'd forgotten about my lack of clothes. "Um . . . I'm travelling light."

"Yeah? You working here?" She winked at me.

"Working? No." Her make-up was blinding me.

"You should think about it," she said. "You could make a lot of money. You sort of have the look for it, you know. And I'm an expert."

Before I could ask what she was talking about, we arrived at the Rio's main entrance. The woman, still clutching my wrist, dragged me down a corridor. We went down some stairs into a dark room that looked like a lounge. People were perched at little cocktail tables.

A huge, beefy man sat at the door, smoking a cigar. At first I cringed – he reminded me of the kind of guy that had attacked both Hiro and me. The kind of guy that I'd had to contend with when Karen was kidnapped. But then I relaxed. He wasn't scoping me out; he barely even looked at me. "Twenty-five," he barked.

I stood there like an idiot. My new stiletto-heeled friend elbowed me. "Pay the guy," she said.

"Oh," I answered. I didn't really want to go to a show unless Katie was working there. I gazed down at the guy. "Does a Katie Riley work here?"

"I don't know," he said gruffly, staring at my black eye. "A lot of girls work here."

"Come on! Pay him!" my friend said to my back. She nudged me. "You're guaranteed to *love* this show. And your Katie's inside. I promise."

I handed over the twenty-five dollars begrudgingly and

walked inside. Just as I found a spot along the wall to lean against (it was *way* too crowded to find a table), a woman glided onstage and announced that the "second act" was starting.

And then all of a sudden about ten guys in tight T-shirts and tight boxer shorts strode out onto the stage. The place went into an uproar. The guys writhed around for a while, grinning. A lot of the women dashed down to the foot of the stage, opening their purses, looking for their wallets.

A woman next to me (not my stiletto friend, who was now missing – maybe she'd gone to find Katie for me) went into something like an apoplectic fit. "Yeah!" she screamed, wriggling and making her minidress fly up and expose her underwear. "Oh my God, I have to get closer," she said, looking at me. She looked absolutely insane. She dashed to the front.

By this time the guys on the stage were simultaneously grinning these thousand-watt smiles and slowly stripping off their clothes.

They were all wearing thongs.

Leopard-print thongs.

My stiletto friend sidled up next to me. "Enjoying yourself?" she asked. "You looked like you needed it, standing there on the street all alone without a man! These Chippendales shows are the best, aren't they?"

Chippendales! Of course! I mean, I'd sort of figured it was *something* like that. I hoped they weren't going to do the full monty. I nodded shakily. "Yeah," I said. One of the guys on the stage stared right at me. He looked just like Colin Farrell. "Whoa," I breathed. Then I turned back to the girl. "He's really hot. So did you find Katie?"

She looked at me blankly. "Who?"

"Take it off!" one of the women screamed.

"Katie Riley," I said over the noise. "The girl I'm looking for."

"Ohhh. Right. You know what? I think I had this place mixed up with another place up the Strip. Sorry." I slumped.

"Shake it!" a woman next to me shouted.

"I come here on my hour off," the woman said, although I hadn't asked. "It's nice to look at *good-looking men*, as opposed to most of the guys I deal with on a daily basis."

She pulled out a mirror and adjusted her lipstick. She had the most amazing lipstick colour I'd ever seen – it seemed to *glow*. I was suspicious of her, no doubt, but the truth was, I needed her.

"Hey, listen," the woman said. "What's your name?"

"Heaven," I answered.

"Rockin' name. Is it real?"

I nodded.

"Mine's Daphne. Like the cute one on *Scooby-Doo*, y'know? What's her name . . . Tara Reid? Anyway, I know of a big party at the Hard Rock pool tonight. You wanna go?"

"Really?" I asked. "But . . . but I don't have a suit." I didn't even have clean *underwear*.

Daphne looked down at me and smiled. "You don't need a bathing suit, silly. It's not a *swimming party*."

"Oh," I said awkwardly. Where was that sassy, snappy Heaven of Vibe? I had to get her back.

But Daphne didn't seem to notice. "So, you in?" she asked. I shrugged but then decided, What the hell?

Daphne said she had to "get back to work," but that I should meet her in front of the Hard Rock casino at 8 p.m. "You won't be disappointed," she said. "You think you can find it okay?"

I nodded.

She winked at me. "Be on time so we can get a good cabana!" She sauntered out of the room.

I gazed up at the writhing men once more. I'd never seen so many guys' butts spinning at once. The women were now starting to climb on the stage and *dance* with the guys. I decided to watch another set. After all, it was a great way to get my mind off Hiro.

3

It was nearing prime Vegas time when I met Daphne for the party. The old lady was right – things *were* much better when the sun wasn't so blinding. Dusk began to fall, and the neon started to twinkle and blink.

As I walked slowly down the strip in what I believed to be the direction of Hard Rock, I did a double take. Was that *Madonna* who'd just walked by? But then I realized – it was Madonna circa *Like a Virgin*. An imposter. Just as I was getting over that shock, three Elvises, arms linked, barrelled past. This place was something.

"You find your friend yet?" Daphne asked as I approached. I shook my head. "Don't worry," she said. "She'll turn up. This is a small town, really. Everyone's connected."

We walked inside through a maze of halls. Finally we came to an open area. Daphne took me by the hand and led me through a set of lavish glass doors. "Check it out," she said, gesturing.

I breathed in. The pool was awesome. It was as big as Hokkaido. It stretched for what seemed like miles. The bluish water lapped calmly in the moonlight. A few people were swimming, but more people were hanging out under little tents – cabanas, I guess – with drinks, talking, laughing. I even saw gambling tables set up right on the water. It was like paradise. And the place was *packed*.

"Come on," Daphne said. "Our cabana party's this way."

We strode to the party area. The people at the pool weren't like people in L.A. in the least – they didn't look you up and down and then walk away. These people were my immediate best friends, although they didn't ask my name or ask to see an ID. They basically didn't care.

Daphne and I walked into the "cabana", which was a big, glowing tent with funky drum-'n'-bass music pulsing from the inside. A girl in nothing but a bikini and sandals greeted us, a huge grin on her face.

"I'm so glad you could come!" she said directly to me. I smiled. I felt a little overdressed: I had on my club gear from working, but everyone else was wearing next to nothing, including the guys.

It was hard to believe that I'd been in L.A., in a *club*, just hours earlier, pouring shots for people. It was hard to believe that my house and all of my stuff had *burned to the ground*. Was Cheryl alive? What was Marcus doing now?

The thoughts swirled quickly to the forefront of my brain. But I shoved them to the back again.

Someone handed me a tall, pink, frothy drink in a beautiful fluted glass.

"It's called a hummingbird," the girl whispered to me. "It'll make your wings flap really fast." I smiled and took it. I didn't remember any drink at Vibe called a hummingbird.

I had vowed not to drink. I'd just made the promise to myself yesterday. I frowned. *This is an extraordinary circumstance,* I thought. So I took a taste. It was like sucking on a giant peach sprinkled in sugar. Delicious. I took another sip.

Daphne sidled up to me. "Don't drink those too fast," she said, a smile creeping onto her lips. "I don't want you to miss finding your friend. Those things can reduce big strong men to puddles."

I stared at the drink again, wondering what was in it. I decided Daphne probably knew what she was talking about, so I put my drink down and watched the dancers. There were tons of girls who might be Katie – beautiful, long-limbed, blonde American girls, girls in good shape, girls with great highlights in their hair, like Katie had. There was even a girl who had the same shoes I'd seen Katie once wear – but I looked at her face and it clearly wasn't her. This girl's face was longer. Katie had a rounder face – sort of heart shaped. I swayed my hips to the beat.

"That's right," a guy wearing an electric yellow Speedo

said. He had a high-pitched voice. He grabbed my hand and started dancing. "I won fifty Gs this morning," he whispered. "I haven't told anyone yet except for you."

I stopped in the middle of the dance floor and had to remember what a G was (it was totally Teddy lingo). Then I remembered: $50,000.

"Wow," I said. "Nice going. What, were you playing the slots or something?" I tried to remember cooler Vegas games (what was the one with the wheel called?) but came up blank.

The guy looked at me. There was something altogether, I don't know . . . *cartoonish* about him. He had on these black-framed glasses, for instance, that were way too big for his face. And he had no muscle tone whatsoever, and he was *shorter* than me. But somehow dancing, wearing his ridiculous bathing suit, wearing that strange knit hat with the earflaps on his head, he seemed, well, *fabulous*. "This is Vegas, sweetie," he said. "This is where dreams come true. Tomorrow I'm gonna see if I can get on *Fear Factor*."

"Do you know Katie Riley?" I blurted.

The guy continued to sway. He didn't answer. I took that as a no. He seemed to be in his own world. I broke off from him, muttering, "Congratulations," and went back to find my drink.

A couple of girls were gathered around the spot where I'd set my drink down.

"Do you really think it's all fake?" said one girl, who had thick brown hair arranged into dreadlocks, a really cool-looking neon green bikini, and about a hundred bracelets snaking up her arm.

Her friend – a Britney Spears look-alike if I'd ever seen one – answered. "I'm *positive*," she said. "She had, like, an exposé on MTV about it!"

I couldn't even fathom what they were talking about and pressed through to find my pink cocktail. The brown-haired girl grabbed me.

"Hey," she said. "Be a part of our poll. Do you think the girl in that Molecule video has been, like, completely lipo-suctioned?"

I looked at them blankly, having no idea who Molecule was. Or maybe she hadn't said Molecule at all.

"Um . . . ," I said. "I don't know. Maybe . . ."

The Britney girl threw her hands up. "You see! Even *she* thinks so!" She looked over at me and smiled.

"Hey – I'm looking for someone," I said. The girls fixed their eyes on me. "Who says she's in Vegas. You guys live around here?"

"I work at the Bellagio," said the dreadlocked girl.

"I work at the Double Down Saloon," said Britney. "What's up?"

"Her name's Katie Riley," I explained. "Does that name sound familiar? She's blonde . . . She's about five-ten . . ."

Britney looked up and held one finger in the air. "I think there's a Katie who works over at the Palms. The place totally got cool after *The Real World* was here. I think I met a girl named Katie who worked there."

"No, Natasha," said the other girl. "You're thinking of *Katrina*. She works at Palms. I don't know anyone named Katie who works there. *But* . . ." She got excited. "There is a Katie who works as a showgirl at Caesars. Oh my God, that's got to be the hardest job, I swear, but I've met her a bunch of times. Blonde, tall. Definitely. She's really cool. Gorgeous, too."

"Oh . . . okay," I said. I couldn't imagine Katie being a showgirl. We used to make up dance routines when we were both a little younger, and I was *always* the stronger dancer. Katie had no sense of rhythm. Plus I just couldn't picture her with a plume atop her head. So I decided I'd stick with the Palms idea.

I found Daphne cuddled up next to my friend in the Speedo. "Hey," I said. "Listen, I have to go look for my friend some more. But . . . thanks for the invite! This was awesome!"

Daphne smiled. "It's too bad you can't stay longer, Heaven." She perked up. "Hey . . . Heaven! Your name is just like the song!"

"What song?" the Speedo guy asked. "Are you in a song?"

I froze. Could she mean . . . ?

"I dunno, it's called . . . 'Heaven's Run Off'? 'Heaven's Gone'?" Daphne said, trying to think.

"Omigod! 'Heaven's Gone'! I love that song!" Speedo guy exclaimed.

*Please tell me I've fallen into the twilight zone.
"Heaven's Gone"?* People were listening to it here, in Vegas?
A. J. back at Vibe had burned me a CD of this hot new group
from Japan called Funkitout. I'd tried to untangle the mystery of why they'd written a song that was completely about
my life but hadn't succeeded. Luckily the words were in
Japanese, but . . .

My heart beat fast. "I haven't heard it," I murmured.

"I only heard it once at a club a couple of days ago,"
Daphne said. "But it's gonna be hot. So is it you?"

I felt sweat creep onto the back of my neck. "Why would
anyone write a song about me?"

The Speedo guy twirled around. "Don't underestimate
yourself, girl!" he squealed.

"Yeah," I said shakily. "Well, it's just a weird coincidence, I guess. Anyway, hope to run into you soon."

"Take my card," Daphne said, reaching into her spangly
bag and pulling out a card. "Call me if you ever want to
party again." She wiggled her fingers in a goodbye. I exited
the cabana and strode quickly alongside the pool. People
were still gambling strong at the floating tables.

When I got out of the hotel, I looked down at the card
Daphne had given me. It said simply:

DAPHNE LARUE
ESCORT SERVICE
WHATEVER YOU'RE INTO!

I stared at it. *Whatever you're into*.

So Daphne was . . . a *hooker*?

Oh God. And she was wondering if . . . *I wanted to be one, too!*

At least she didn't know who I *really* was.

I went into the Monte Carlo, which had a gigantic green fountain in front of it and a bunch of steps to climb. The lobby was immaculate – shiny floors, beautiful woodwork, comfortable furniture.

I walked up to the desk. But before I could approach the woman behind the counter, I felt a hand on my shoulder. I flinched, turned around, and was inches away from round-house kicking a scrawny guy with oversized glasses and thinning hair.

"Whoa!" he said, jumping back. "Don't hurt me! I was going to ask you to marry me!"

I stared at him. "What?"

He gestured into the hotel. "There's a wedding chapel here. I was supposed to marry someone else, but she can-celled on me. Just walked out! But I put down the deposit . . . and it's so depressing to have to ask for it back . . ." His eyes searched over me. He was wearing a tuxedo, fully prepared to marry. "You're so beautiful," he said desperately. I looked down at myself. I was wearing a filthy T-shirt and low-rider jeans, I'd been sitting on a bus, I'd *slept* in them, and I'd spilled half of my pink drink down the front of my shirt. I wore no make-up, and I was sure my hair looked like it had been caught in a hurricane. "Uh-huh," I said, and started to walk away.

"No!" the guy continued. "They do a Japanese service and everything . . . I mean, if you are Japanese and don't speak English . . . Please . . . I just need to get married . . . I don't even mind about your eye . . . I'd never hurt you . . ."

I turned back to him, flinching at the reference to my eye. I'd definitely have to put make-up on it. "I'm sorry," I said. "But I'm already engaged." His shoulders drooped, but then I saw his attention turn to another woman who had walked in, also looking quite lost. I giggled to myself and then frowned.

I went up to the desk and shrugged and tried to laugh. "I'm looking for the Palms casino," I said in a low voice.

"He's not gonna follow you," the woman murmured. "He's in here every day, askin' women to marry him."

"Can't you just ask him to leave?" I asked.

The woman shrugged. "Are you kidding me? He's a whale."

"A whale?" I asked.

"Major gambler," she whispered. "We're talking millions." She looked around, then straightened up. "You want the Palms? Pass the Bellagio, turn, walk a little farther. It's off on a side street, but you'll see it as you approach." She wrote down the address on a slip of paper.

"Thanks," I said. I slunk out of the hotel. The whale was trying to convince another Japanese girl sitting on one of the couches that she was the love of his life.

I walked down the street to the Palms. I'd watched some of *The Real World Las Vegas* when it was on, so I recognized the sign. I went cautiously through the glass doors and found my way to the bar. If there was anyone who knew where Katie was, it would probably be the bartender. I could sit at the bar, relax, have a proper drink, and hopefully talk to someone about where Katie might be.

Quiet experience? Um, no. I pushed through the doors of the Ghost Bar and could hardly get inside. The place was *jam-packed* with people. Everyone was dancing. I shoved my way to the bar and sat down.

I was getting nervous. It was early yet, but would I find Katie?

I finally snagged the bartender and ordered a drink. Then I said, "I'm looking for Katie Riley."

"What?" he asked.

"I'M LOOKING FOR KATIE RILEY!" I screamed. Behind me, someone apparently had taken off her top. The bartender put his hands over his head and screamed. I sat back down on the stool.

A cocktail waitress pushed by. I asked her the same question. She looked annoyed that I'd stopped her.

"Don't know any Katie Riley, sorry," she said, and hurried on. The couple next to me started to do body shots.

I gritted my teeth. Why had I expected to find Katie in this town of a million partyers?

I stared wistfully at the television. They were playing reruns of *The Real World Las Vegas. How cheesy,* I thought. *So dumb to show the TV show set in your own hotel in your hotel's bar.* The guy next to me – the one who'd been doing body shots with some girl who was now not at the bar – poked me with his elbow.

"This one's a classic," he said. "This is the one where the two chicks hook up and then they bring the guy into it. You seen it?"

"Uh, no," I said. I stared at the TV. Maybe I *had* seen this one. The scene cut to a commercial for some bar in some hotel. There was a shot of a couple dancing and people drinking big fizzy yellow drinks. *Cheesy,* I thought. But then I saw something in the background. I sat up straight.

There was Katie. On TV. In the background. Tending bar. *Tending bar!*

My mouth dropped open. I squinted. I couldn't believe it. It really *was* Katie! It was definitely her! She was even wearing the hair clips that I'd given her for her birthday! My heart started to pound. The words *Rum Jungle* flashed across the scene. I grabbed the bartender. "Is Rum Jungle in Vegas?" I screamed, pointing at the screen.

The bartender squinted and shrugged. Then another shot flickered in front of the screen. Some outside scene. "Oh, that's over at Mandalay Bay," he said.

I dug through my purse and threw down much more money than needed.

"Thanks," I yelled, and quickly elbowed my way out of the bar.

Back on the Strip, I stopped a guy dressed as Elvis.

"Mandalay Bay," I muttered, out of breath. "Which way?" He pointed, and I dashed off. I swear I got there in like a minute flat. I ran into the hotel lobby and asked directions to the bar.

The woman looked a little confused. "Which bar?" she said. "We have several . . ."

For the life of me I couldn't remember the name. "I don't know," I said, frustrated, waving my arms around. "Clubby . . . dark, sorta. Lots of trendy people . . . ? Maybe . . . Rain Forest or something?"

"Oh, you mean Rum Jungle." She smiled and pointed me on my way.

I dashed inside. The room smelled like coconuts. The music was pretty cool – some crazy African beat. It was wall-to-wall with dancers.

But Katie wasn't behind the bar.

I mean, this was definitely the bar in the commercial. No doubt about it. It looked exactly the same. But there were two guys and one girl quickly stirring and shaking and pouring. No Katie.

I checked my watch again: 1 a.m. This place was going to close soon for sure. I sat down and tried to think. But then I looked up and saw a girl in a high ponytail and famil-iar-looking clips come out from some back room. She had a bag slung over her shoulder and looked ready to leave.

"Katie!" I screamed. The girl looked up. It was her.

She looked absolutely stunned when she saw me. "Heaven?" she said. She looked me up and down. "Oh my God!" she cried. I couldn't tell if it was a good "oh my God" or a worried one. I smiled shakily. "How did you find me?" she asked.

"By watching *Real World*," I said, and giggled. "You were on a commercial!"

Katie shook her head a little – I'd definitely bowled her over. Finally she gave me a huge hug.

"Oh my God," she repeated. Maybe I was crazy, but a look of worry crossed over her face. "I thought . . . ," she started, but then just shook her head. "Wow," she said.

I couldn't quite believe it, either. I didn't even know what to say. I realized tears were streaming down my cheeks. "I – I had to get out of L.A.," I said. "This was the only place I could think of." The words were spilling from my mouth too fast for me to realize what I was saying.

"I heard about your father," Katie said. "He's in a coma?"

"Yes," I said. "He's still in a coma, as far as I know. The doctors say he might recover soon . . . I don't know. I mean, maybe. I don't know much."

"It's really you," Katie said, hugging me. But by this

point I was wiping my eyes, trying to pull myself together. I broke away from her and smiled.

"You look the same," I said. "How have you been doing?"

"Oh, okay," she said quickly. "But . . . Heaven, I heard about your wedding. Sort of through the grapevine. And then . . . I tried to call your house in Japan . . . a bunch of times . . . but no one answered, not even Harumi. I left all kinds of messages, but no one called me back."

That's because they didn't have anything to tell you, I thought. I quickly explained what had happened – Ohiko, Teddy, Hiro, the attacks, kidnappings, the fire, everything. As I explained, Katie's face became more and more worried – more and more freaked out.

Finally, when I finished, she said, "I've been so worried about you, Heaven. For good reason! But you seem so strong! And buff!" She looked me up and down.

"Hiro and I were doing some . . . uh . . . jujitsu and stuff," I said. I didn't know if I wanted to get into all of the samurai deal. "Self-defense," I explained. "It's actually helped a lot. To clear my mind."

"You're so brave," Katie said. The club-goers swirled around us.

Katie and I sat down in the back room and I continued to talk for another hour. Katie was such a good listener – it was a relief to finally *tell* someone all this stuff!

I admitted my feelings for Hiro. And how crushed I'd

49

been to find out that he was interested in someone else. I explained how he'd just dumped me off at the bus station but also how strangely he'd been acting.

"What do you think he meant by, 'My feelings for you are very strong . . . You don't understand'?" I asked.

"Maybe he secretly likes you," Katie said. I shook my head. Fat chance. "Look, you have to come back to my house and get some sleep," she continued. "I can't believe you were on a *bus* half the night. And . . . that you lost all your stuff! Of course" – she smiled – "we can fix that." I smiled back. Katie and I had always been the same size. But then a concerned look floated over her face, sort of the same one I'd seen when we'd first hugged. "Are you sure it's safe here? What if they come looking for you?"

"Well, the only person who knew I was coming here was Hiro," I said. "No one followed us to the bus station, and I don't think Hiro will be telling anyone where I've gone." I cleared my throat and said the next part in a low voice, more to myself. "I don't think Hiro will be thinking about me much at all."

Katie pulled me up. "In that case, you can stay with me as long as you want. I mean, you should totally get a job here. How fun would that be? And we can go out together!" Her eyes sparkled. "Without having to worry about sneaking around."

"Totally," I said.

"Come on, let's get you home," Katie said. "I'm sure you're exhausted."

"You know, I'm actually not," I said. "I'm pretty wide awake, to tell you the truth. You wanna do something?"

Katie looked at me strangely. "Are you *sure*?" she asked.

"Seriously," I said. "Let's go clubbing or something. Show me around!" I spread my arms out wide.

Katie looked at me, astounded. "Heaven," she said incredulously, "it's really late . . . and you seem awfully relaxed for someone who's been through . . . so much."

I shrugged. I couldn't exactly explain to Katie that the less I dwelled on things, the better. Plus no one was watching me right now. Not my father. Not Mieko. Not Teddy. Not Hiro. I didn't have to answer to anyone, to explain myself. "I want to move around," I told Katie. "I want to dance!"

"Well, all right," Katie said slowly. "If that's what you want, that's what we'll do!"

Blown in like a tumbleweed. "Hi, Katie! I found you by watching The Real World!*"*

I mean, don't get me wrong. It's great to see Heaven. I never thought I'd see her again. But . . . I'm worried. For her . . . and for me.

I knew things she didn't.

And I wasn't allowed to tell her.

It was why I spoke out against her wedding and sepa-rated myself from the Kogo family.

One evening, only a few days after Heaven's engage-ment was announced, I was sneaking in from a date I'd had with Yatsumi. We'd gone to see another American movie – Blue Crush. *I was coming in through the back, and I saw Konishi try to open the door with blood all over his shirt and hands. It was disgusting; it shone a violent red in the back porch light. I wondered why no one was letting him in. He struggled with his key.*

"Kogo-san," I said. "What is wrong?"

He froze in his tracks. He gave me a look that was so ter-rifying, I turned and ran in the other direction. What is going on? *I thought.* What did I just see?

I managed to get inside a few hours later. My whole body shook the entire night.

The next day Mieko came to see me. She spoke very qui-etly. "You have seen things," she said. She stared at me. I didn't know what to say. So I just nodded.

She continued. "But they are not what they seem. You

must forget them. And you must never tell Heaven. If you do, you must leave immediately. Is that understood?"

It was the only time Mieko had ever sounded even vaguely *aggressive*. I nodded silently.

"You must not see Yatsumi anymore," she continued, her eyes steely. "Do not ask questions."

"What?" I asked.

"You will never understand," she said. And then she left.

A few weeks later, after the first Teddy-Heaven engagement party, I went to a café in Harajuku with Heaven and one of the bodyguards. They were both in the bathroom or something; I was the only one at the table. My friend Kenji, who sometimes worked at the Kogos' with Yatsumi, sat down and stared at me. I looked at him and my heart started beating faster. The look on his face told me I had something to worry about.

"What is it?" I asked.

"Yatsumi is dead," he said softly. "Don't ask me how I know, but I know. He is."

"What?" I said.

"You know who they are, right? The Kogos? You know what it's all about?" I nodded dumbly. I did. I did know. "Yatsumi tried to be involved . . . Perhaps he got too close. I don't know."

Kenji darted away as Heaven and the bodyguard came back to sit down. "Why are you shaking?" Heaven asked. I told her I was cold.

The next day I spoke out against her wedding. And the Kogos asked me to leave. If they'd had to ask again, I doubt they would've asked nicely.

I was afraid for Heaven. I knew something was going to happen. Something that wasn't good. When I read about the attacks at Heaven's wedding, my heart dropped. I prayed that she was okay. I wished I could've done something to help her.

But now she's here. What do I do? What if they come looking for her?

I can't get Konishi Kogo's face and the blood all over his body out of my head.

Katie

4

Katie opened up her cell phone and then stopped. "Heaven, are you sure you want to go *out*? If you're being attacked by random people . . . don't you feel like you'll be in a lot of danger?"

"No, I want to hit the clubs for a little bit," I said. "C'mon, Katie! Don't tell me you usually go *home* most nights after working!"

Katie shrugged. "Well, it's true, a lot of times I don't . . ." She trailed off. "Listen, at *least* put on some kind of disguise – like a wig or something. Can you do that?"

"Katie, I don't know anyone here," I said. "Honest. And no one saw me get on the bus." I saw Katie's face grow worried and held up my hand. "Okay. How about I just get a funky hat and some sunglasses? That's all I'll need." I pulled her arm. "Let's go look! I saw some late night crazy accessories places still open up the street."

"Okay . . . ," Katie answered, hanging back. But quickly she was walking next to me. "I just can't believe you're here," she said. "This is just so unbelievable."

"Well, believe it, baby!" I said. "I'm here!"

We found the accessories place I was talking about – it had lots of I Love Vegas T-shirts and silly glasses and lots of strange Elvis stuff. I picked up a newsboy sort of hat, the kind J.Lo always wears. "How does this look?" I asked Katie.

"Good," she answered. She put on a really glitzy, ridiculous top hat. Some of the sparkles fell off on her sleeve. The lighting in the place was terrible – black lights, almost. You couldn't even really see what you looked like. And techno music boomed from some invisible speakers. I grabbed some wraparound yellow-tinted sunglasses from the rack and put them on.

"Here we go," I said. "Perfect for clubbing."

"Let me figure out what place is good tonight," Katie said, opening her phone again. She quickly dialled a number and started talking to someone on the other end. "It's Katie!" she said in a high-pitched voice, smiling. "Yeah . . . yeah . . . what? Cool! That sounds perfect. Yeah, I've got a friend from out of town. So where is it? Free drinks? Cool." She looked up at me. "You can get us comped . . . ? Yeah, there's me and then my friend Heaven." She looked up again, smiled, and flashed me a thumbs-up sign.

An amazing feeling washed over me. *You're the woman,*

I told myself. *Look what you've just done. You've found Katie. You don't need anyone else.* Indeed. I'd got on a bus and come to a new city without knowing anyone. And I'd found my oldest friend, after meeting a hooker and a lot of other weird characters in the process.

"So where's the party?" I asked Katie.

"It's at Baby's, but we'd better get done up before we go out," Katie said. She held up her purse and shook it. "I've got a *ton* of make-up in here. Same stuff as always!"

Katie and I used to give each other makeovers with her huge collection of make-up. She would dump it all out on my carpet and I'd marvel over the different wands and brushes and eye shadows and lipsticks. It was just like a regular sleepover, except Katie was *good*. I was a little surprised that she hadn't gone into make-up artistry when she'd gone back to the States. I could see her being a stylist on a music video shoot. Going on tour with Beyoncé or something.

We walked into Caesars Palace in search of a bathroom. Katie took me by the hand, winding through the glitzy corridors to find "the bigger bathroom with the better mirrors".

"How do you know the inside of this place so well?"

"I've been to a bunch of parties here," Katie said.

I thought about this. Katie and I had been separated only a little while, and she already knew Vegas like the back of her hand. She must have partied every night.

We reached the luxurious bathroom and Katie sat down on one of the sofas that were positioned in front of a large mirror. "Oh my God, I didn't even notice your eye!" she said, putting a hand up to her mouth.

"It's no big deal," I said.

Katie stared at me for a few minutes, not saying anything.

"Really," I said. "Don't worry about it." I stared at myself in the mirror. "Whoa, not too pretty!" I said, trying to be flip. My eye had turned a hideous purplish blue.

Katie still was quiet. It seemed like she wanted to say something but kept stopping herself.

"Can you cover it up?" I asked nonchalantly.

"Of course . . . ," Katie said, trailing off. She opened her make-up bag and took out a bunch of foundation bottles, powder compacts, moisturizers, glitter tubes, and self-tanners. "Does it hurt?" she asked, spreading a foundation cream on my eye.

"A little," I said.

We didn't say anything for a bit. I wondered what was going through Katie's mind.

"Your skin as a whole looks really clear," Katie said. "You said you've been working out?"

"Sort of," I said. "With Hiro. Martial arts stuff."

"Working out always helps," Katie murmured. I heard her take the cap off something and then felt a pressure on my eyelashes. "Honestly, Heaven, you don't even need that much make-up except for this eye . . . and you look so buff . . . It totally gives you sex appeal."

"Put glitter on me," I said, looking at the bottle. "Give me *more* sex appeal!"

I felt her putting the eyeliner on me and then felt a cool tube on my lips. "Okay, open," she said, giggling.

I opened my eyes. They looked *insane*. I looked like a crazed cat with coral pink lips. *And* my black eye was gone. "Whoa," I said. "I'm ready for my close-up." Katie had put so much eyeliner on herself that the rest of her face looked deathly pale in comparison. Except her lips – she put a strange bluish-red lipstick on them.

I grabbed a tissue and started wiping it all off. I caught a glimpse of my face in the mirror, framed by my new hat. I pulled it to one side and slouched my trousers down past my hips. I tapped Katie. "Yo, yo," I said in a deep voice. "I'm Teddy Yukemura."

Katie and I cracked up. "Teddy Yukemura with coral lipstick!"

"Teddy Yukemura in drag!" I burst into laughter. I thought of Teddy carefully putting on lipstick and at the same time making sure his trousers were pulled down precisely enough so he looked like a "gangsta". The thought made me laugh even harder.

When I calmed down somewhat, Katie said, "Hey, if you want to change out of that T-shirt, I've got an extra tube top in my bag." She fished around and found a simple black tube top with tiny silvery threads running through it. She tossed it to me. "How's that?"

I tried it on, pulled up my trousers, and looked at myself in the mirror. "Not bad," I said.

Katie stepped back. "Check you out!" she squealed.

I did a few bodybuilder-type flexing moves. "I'm so glad we're going out," I said. "Remember how my dad used to be about this stuff? We were completely trapped!"

"God, yeah," Katie said. "Remember when we went out just to get some movies, but we went to that sort of indie movie place in Roppongi, and your father freaked out that we were going there because he thought we were going to go to a club?"

"Yeah," I groaned.

"And he sent one of the guys he worked with . . . what was his name? Taru? He sent him to *follow* us! And there was Taru on the train, there was Taru in the video store . . . and you were finally like . . ."

"I finally confronted him and asked what he was doing," I said. "And he said he wanted to watch some movies. And he was holding the box for the first season of *Sex and the City*!" I exploded into laughter again. "And when he looked down and realized what it was . . ."

"Oh God, he got soooo embarrassed!" Katie hooted. "So then we took a very looonnnnng way home and nearly got lost!"

I took a deep breath and turned to Katie. "So . . . did you know that my father was involved in . . . some pretty rough stuff?"

Katie stopped reapplying her make-up. "Um, well, maybe. I don't know," she said in Japanese. She didn't look me straight in the eye.

"Yakuza," I said. Katie nodded.

I took a deep breath. "After everything happened at my wedding, I started to really wonder about who my father is. So I did some research on him. And then . . . there was this guy at this cybercafé I worked at . . ." I told her how I'd extracted the information from another yakuza member at Life Bytes, the cybercafé I'd worked at for only a day.

"I also found out that Teddy's involved," I said.

"Really," Katie said. She didn't seem very surprised.

"Yeah," I said. "Apparently it was some deal struck between his family and mine . . . for money. Or something."

Katie put all her make-up back in her bag silently.

"Did you *know* this stuff?" I asked her.

"Well, no," Katie said. "Or . . . I don't know. I mean, no. I didn't know about Teddy." She smiled faintly. "Teddy really *is* a gangsta."

"But . . . well, he's not that bad," I said. "I've been through some stuff with Teddy lately that makes me think *he's* not all bad. His father, maybe."

"I don't know," Katie said. "From what you've told me, Teddy seems pretty horrible. I mean, I met him that one time, at one of your engagement parties? *Totally* slimy."

"Yeah . . ." I drifted off, wanting to change the subject. "Really, my mind keeps circling back to Mieko . . . but I don't know why."

"Mieko?" Katie laughed. "I mean, she was a little weird, but she looked like she wouldn't hurt a fly. She was afraid of everything, remember? She was afraid of *squirrels*."

I considered this. Mieko *was* deathly afraid of squirrels. She also had a weird thing about cleanliness, thinking we were all going to come down with some crazy infectious disease.

"Still," I said. "Something about her . . ." I explained the phone call, Marcus, and the fire.

"I can't quite see Mieko, like, plotting stuff out. A mastermind." She had sort of a pensive look on her face all of a sudden. "Although . . . ," she said quietly.

There was a silence. "Although what?" I said.

"Nothing," she said.

"Little Mieko, threatening my life," I continued. "But my house burned down just days after I'd spoken to her. Isn't that a strange coincidence?"

"But if Mieko *is* behind it and doesn't want you to know that it's her, why would she do something like that? It seems too obvious," Katie said. "She must know you're a smart girl. That you'd figure it out. If she didn't, she majorly underestimated you. I mean, is she that stupid? Really?"

"Maybe," I said. Katie's voice was awfully high-pitched

all of a sudden. I looked at her, my face squashed up. "Is there something you *do* know that you aren't telling me?" I asked her.

Katie didn't answer. *"What?"* I asked. "Did they . . . *do* something to you or something?"

"Don't worry about it," Katie said. "It was nothing. I just knew your dad wasn't into good stuff, that's all."

What did she know? Why hadn't she ever told me?

And then, all at once, even though it totally wasn't what I wanted to discuss, I blurted, "Hey, whatever happened to Yatsumi?"

Katie stopped what she was doing. "Huh?" she said.

"Yatsumi," I said again. "I know you went out with him a couple of times. You know, the really cute gardener? You dated him right around when I got engaged . . . Whatever happened with him?"

"Oh . . . ," Katie said. "Um, I don't know. We didn't keep in touch."

"Really? Did you just not care about him anymore or what?" I said.

"I . . . guess not," Katie said.

"You know, I really liked him," I said, not looking at her. "I was really jealous of you for going out with him. For being *able* to go out with him. And now you've, like, not even kept in touch with him?" I sighed.

"Why didn't you ever tell me you liked him?" Katie asked. She still wouldn't quite look me in the eye.

"I thought I did," I said.

"You didn't," Katie said. She took a deep breath. "Besides, he's dead. I guess I can tell you that now. *That's* why I didn't keep in touch with him."

I looked at her. "He's dead?"

Katie nodded. "I don't know how it happened, though. I just know he's dead."

She crossed her arms, as if to say that the conversation was finished. "I'm sorry I hurt you. I had no idea. But . . . I'm hurt, too. I don't want him to be dead. I liked him. I haven't had a boyfriend in ages. It was weird being a blonde, white girl in Japan, you know?" She sighed.

I nodded. Sort of like being a sheltered Japanese girl in L.A. We both stood, looking in the mirror in silence.

"He's *dead*?" I asked. Katie nodded again. "Is it because of . . . my father?"

Katie's head didn't move. She stared at me in the mirror. "You couldn't have survived as long as you have and not learned the truth."

"Wow," I said, breathing in nervously. "For what it's worth, I'm sorry."

Finally Katie straightened up. "Listen, let's not think about this now. That's behind us, right? Let's go party."

I straightened up, too. "You're right," I said. I smiled at her. I had to try and shake this weird feeling for the night, but I knew it would most likely stay at the back of my mind for the remainder of the day and probably into tomorrow.

Katie wasn't as naive as I'd thought. And I had a feeling she was tougher than I'd thought, too.

The party was at Baby's, back at the Hard Rock. "I've already been here once tonight!" I proclaimed to Katie. We had to climb a spiral staircase to even get to the club, but I could hear the beat pounding away. Judging from the people who were going inside, I thought it seemed like a hip spot to be.

"You on the list?" a big guy asked us as we strode up to the entrance. Katie gave our names and the guy opened the rope and ushered us inside. We had to go through a couple of metal detectors and a pat down before we even saw the inside of the place.

Katie and I walked in and saw a huge dance floor, spinning lights, and various twisty staircases. People were everywhere.

"What do you think?" Katie asked.

"It's great!" I said. I could hear different music coming out of different little dancing rooms we passed. One had hardcore house, where kids with light sticks and baggy Adidas trousers thrashed away; the next had ambient stuff, where people sat on sofas, drinking cocktails. Women in leathery zippered shirts passed, taking drink orders. The place looked like something out of a James Bond movie. Something by Royksopp was playing on the main dance floor.

"So . . . you want to get a drink?" Katie asked. I nodded.

Katie walked up to the bartender and smiled. "Hey, Cleo," she said. The girl behind the bar waved. "What do you want to drink, Heaven?"

"Um . . . maybe a lemon drop?" I asked, trying to conjure up my knowledge of drinks. I'd had to pour a lot of lemon drops as the Vibe shot girl.

"A lemon drop?" Katie said wryly. "You don't really want a *shot*, do you? Let's get sexy drinks, like cosmos or something!"

"Okay," I said. I'd never tried a cosmo before, but I liked the idea of holding the long-stemmed glass and slowly sipping. Perhaps it would make me look ultrasexy.

I remembered my anti-alcohol vow again. This was drink number two. *Screw it,* I immediately thought. *You're not in L.A. anymore.*

"Two cosmos," Katie said to the bartender. She turned back to me. "Sex in Sin City! We're going to find you a man tonight, Heaven!" she said, smiling. Cleo made our drinks and set them in front of us – they looked delicious. Katie waved a twenty at Cleo, but she shook her head. "On the house," she mouthed. Katie smiled in thanks. I leaned against the bar with mine and sipped. The drink was great – sorta like the peachy one I'd had earlier at the pool party.

The DJ switched records, and I heard strains of something familiar layered over a basic drum track. It was sped up and sort of garbled, but I knew what it was right away.

"Heaven's Gone."

I broke into a cold sweat. I couldn't believe it. What was this song doing on?

First Daphne and Speedo guy . . . now this club?

"Heaven?" Katie looked at me inquisitively. "What is it?"

"Um . . . nothing," I said. My hands were shaking. The dancers on the floor were going crazy.

"You look kinda pale . . ."

"I'm okay," I insisted. How popular was this song going to get? How long until MTV got ahold of it and translated it? Was my face soon going to be plastered all over *Us Weekly*? My head started to spin. Katie bounced her head to the music but looked like she wasn't listening very carefully to the words. It seemed that she didn't know the song at all. I took a quick look around the club but didn't notice anyone Japanese or even Asian. Was it possible no one noticed? Was it possible I was just totally paranoid?

I gulped down my drink.

The "Heaven" song ended quickly. The DJ kept the drumbeat going and put on a new song. It was one from Madonna's *American Life*. They'd layered it into a clubby, dreamy sort of song. I started to sway, really feeling the energy of the music.

I opened my eyes and noticed a lot of people around me dancing together, looking into each other's eyes, making out. I frowned. I couldn't help but think of Hiro. I recalled those brief moments Hiro and I had shared in the cab, just before we discovered my place was on fire. And what had he meant by "You don't understand . . ."?

"C'mon," I said to Katie, swilling my drink. "Let's go dance." We sauntered out to the dance floor. "I'm wallowing in Hiro misery," I told her.

"You really love him, huh?" Katie asked.

"I do," I said. Despite myself, I was choking back tears again. "I've done my best to put it out of my head and I'm so happy that I found you, but honestly, I'm just so heartbroken right now . . ."

Katie grabbed me and gave me a huge hug. "I'm sorry," she said. Then she took me by the shoulders. "Look, this is why we have to find you a man for the night! Now, come on." She led me onto the dance floor.

We'd been dancing for a while when I noticed two guys watching us. They stood on the edge of the floor, their arms crossed. Katie nudged me.

"See?" she said. "They're hot! Let's get them to come over!"

Eventually Katie took one of the guys' hands and dragged him out onto the floor. The other one followed quickly and came up to me. He moved very close to me for a while, our bodies not touching but dancing in unison. Finally he put his hand lightly around my waist. We did that for a while, and then he whispered into my ear, "I'm Mike."

"I'm Heaven," I said, trying to sound sexy and not like I was screaming over the throbbing bass.

"You sure are!" he said, this not quite coming out a pickup line, but more a blurting of the truth. I'd heard the "heavenly" metaphor before. "You wanna sit down for a little bit?"

Mike – tall, brown hair, deep, soulful eyes, black shirt, nice-fitting Diesel jeans – led me back to the bar. "Another drink?" he asked. I nodded.

We sat with our drinks and tried to have a conversation over the noise. "So, let me guess," he said. "You're an actress."

"That's right!" I said. What else could I say? "Well, really I'm more of a dancer, but I'd like to get into acting. I've even had a couple of auditions." I didn't know where these lies were coming from. But once I got started, it was pretty easy.

"You had some great dance moves out there," Mike said, eyeing my drink. "You need another drink?" I looked down. My drink was gone. Had I drunk it that fast? My head was starting to spin. I had to slow down. "Sure," I said, promising myself I'd pace myself with drink number three.

"You're beautiful," Mike said. "Girls like you don't come in here that often. And I know. I work over at New York, New York – and you are a rare breed, let me tell you."

"You're making me sound like a dog," I said. I had a feeling I was getting a little too tipsy. That joke, as soon as I said it, sounded like the most hilarious thing I'd ever heard in the world. I tipped my head back and started laughing. Mike looked at me funny, then started laughing, too.

"Have you ever been to New York?" he asked me. "The real place, I mean. Not the casino."

"No," I said. Was I slurring my words? "But my father used to go there a lot."

"Oh, yeah? Who's your father?"

"My father is . . . my father is . . ." I chugged the rest of my drink – I couldn't exactly help myself at this point. "Come on," I said seductively. "I want to dance." I took Mike by the wrist and led him back onto the dance floor (*Hiro, just look at me now!*), where Katie and her guy were wound in a tight embrace. The DJ switched songs again to a sexy, ambient one. The lights dimmed even further. I could feel the heat thrown off by the other bodies around us – the air was humid and charged. I put my arms around Mike. He looked down at me. And then, all at once, before I could quite control it, we started to kiss.

Now, for how long we made out I had no idea. It seemed like hours. It also seemed like seconds. But even in my drunken state my senses were ultraheightened. Every part of my body felt awesome. Here I was, making out with a gorgeous guy (with no strings attached) at a Vegas club. I felt like a balloon set free in the air.

Oh, and he was a good kisser, too.

We finally broke free. "Heaven," Mike whispered in my ear. I realized that the room was spinning slightly and that I really had to go to the bathroom. Katie was getting tired, too, so we all headed back to the bar again. "Another cosmo?" Katie asked me. I looked at her wearily. I'd had three times the alcohol she'd had tonight. "Sure," I said. "Order me one." I headed in the direction of the bathroom.

It was probably about 2 a.m. now, and the crowd was getting superthick. I had to really shove my way through people to get to the bathroom. I looked around me and realized that this place looked a lot like the swinging club scene in *Austin Powers* – sorta retro, girls in leather outfits, people in skinny, tight miniskirts. Free.

Finally I saw the women's bathroom in the distance. There wasn't even a line to it. I wavered a little as I wove to the door but didn't feel sick or anything. I just felt giddy and a little dizzy. "I rock!" I whispered to myself, giggling. I couldn't believe I'd just made out with someone on the dance floor. "Go, me!" I whispered. No one could hear me, anyway – the noise was deafening.

I turned the corner and a hand shot out to stop me. "Hey!" I said, possibly internally. My body tensed up.

My first thought was: *Marcus found me. He drove the whole way here and found me.*

But when I turned around, it wasn't Marcus. I was staring at Teddy Yukemura.

┌─────┐
│ 5 │
└─────┘

There was Teddy, looking down at me.

I thought I'd seen him at Vibe, too, but that had turned out to be a mirage. But here he was, right in front of me. He mouthed something, although it was way too loud to hear anything he was saying. His face looked excited – happy, even. A little shocked but actually pretty . . . stoked.

My gut said, *Throw him to the ground.*

Wait. I hesitated. The alcohol was confusing me. Teddy had helped me not too long ago. If he hadn't intervened, Karen could be dead or . . . we'd be married.

I'd even decided that it would be a *good thing* to see Teddy – at least with him, I'd have nothing to hide.

Finally Teddy screamed loud enough for me to hear him. "Ay yo trip!" he said, waving his arms around, widening his eyes, seeing if it was really me. "This is *bizzo*!"

Ok, this had to be a dream. First off, Teddy was just *too* stereotypically Teddy. *Ay yo trip?!? Bizzo!?* And he was wearing his low-rider trousers, boxers hanging out, a huge Echo Unlimited sweatshirt with a hood, Armani Exchange ball cap on sideways. I mean, come on. Teddy was supposed to be in hiding. Wearing dark glasses, maybe changing his hair around or something, right? He looked the same as he always had. When I'd thought I saw him at Vibe, he'd been dressed like this. "Heaven Kiz-ogo!" Teddy said, this time not so loud.

Wow. It definitely *was* Teddy.

It seemed like all the alcohol hit me at once. I honestly didn't know what to do. My head spun. I felt unsteady on my feet. My mouth crinkled itself up into something that resembled a smile, but my brain felt absolutely scrambled. The hamburger I'd eaten about one bite of hours ago churned in my stomach. And still my adrenaline raced   *Throw him to the ground,* my gut said. I blinked a couple of times, shook my head. Teddy stood there, waiting. People streamed by us. I considered my options. If I ran away, he'd follow me. I'd have to say something.

"Teddy . . . ," I said slowly, "you're . . . you're in Vegas!"

That was really all I could muster.

"What are *you* doing here?" he asked. But he wasn't shady or surly about it. He seemed honestly ecstatic. "Isn't this place great? It has the best parties . . ."

"I'm . . . I found Katie," I said. "Katie, my tutor, remember?" I continued. "In Japan? She lives here now."

"Oh, yeah, word?" Teddy said, grinning. Why wasn't he cagier about seeing me? Unless he'd had a bunch of drinks, too . . . Oh God, the two of us putting ourselves in danger, having this conversation . . . both of us drunk . . .

"You want to say hi?" I asked. My words and actions were slipping beyond my control. The cosmopolitans had taken over. Even my vision was now frothy pink. It was like I was still sexy Heaven, the dancer-actress in L.A., a regular girl hanging out in Vegas to have some fun, not to flee some invisible enemy. But more than that, what could I do? Now that I'd seen Teddy, I would have to talk to him. It was likely that he'd follow me, anyway. Teddy had a keen ability to track people, even if he wasn't the brightest person in the world. I took his hand. "Come on. Let's go."

We threaded through the crowd to where Katie was standing with the guy she'd been dancing with, Steve. They were talking with Mike, and they all turned around, quite surprised, when I returned with a hulking, gangsta-rap Asian guy with bleached blond hair. He looked like my bodyguard.

"Guys, this is Teddy," I screamed over the music. "He's an old friend."

"What's up," Teddy said, extending not his hand but his closed fist. Mike and Steve looked at him, confused, and finally just nodded. Teddy shrugged and stuffed his hands in his pockets, surveying the scene.

"I know you," Katie said. Immediately she pulled me aside and spoke quietly. "Heaven," she said. "What is he doing here? What the hell? You said no one would be here that you knew, and . . . are you in danger? Why are you hanging around with him?"

"I don't know what he's doing here," I said, slurring my words a little. "He's hiding from his dad, I think." I giggled, thinking about a little kid Teddy hiding under the dining-room table from his father. Not that Teddy and I had been friends when we were kids or anything. I could just imagine it. Teddy was such a wimp when it came to his father.

"But . . . God, Heaven, isn't it dangerous to be around him?" Katie asked, wide-eyed. "And don't you *hate* him?" She was hysterical. "What if . . . what if he sends people to *attack* you?"

"That won't happen," I said, giving her a playful punch. My other personality, sexy Heaven, had definitely taken over for good. "He helped me out of a kidnapping . . ." God, I could sort of hear myself from way inside my head. I sounded a little insane. But the truth was, I did trust Teddy. This wasn't all a drunken act; I didn't even consider it a mistake. It was freaky that he was here, but in a way, I was glad to know he wasn't dead. I knew this would be a very difficult thing to explain to Katie, especially since I'd told her Teddy was part of the yakuza.

75

"We were almost married!" I said gleefully. "Can you believe that? Me almost married?" I hummed the wedding march song: "DUH duh duh duh!" Katie looked at me suspiciously.

I felt a hand on my shoulder and turned. Teddy loomed above me, huge. I saw Mike and Steve in the background, looking completely confused. "Hey," Teddy said. "I don't think I've met your fly friend here."

"This is the Katie I've been telling you about," I said. "*Isn't* she fly? I was just thinking that myself."

"Oh God," Katie said, rolling her eyes, careful not to look at him. "I believe you said the same thing to me at one of your engagement parties."

"I don't think I ever met you," Teddy said. "I'd remember. Heaven never told me that her tutor was such a honey."

"We *did* meet," Katie said in an icy voice. She looked back and forth awkwardly from Steve to Mike to Teddy. She shrugged to the boys.

"Listen, I've got access to the VIP room," Teddy said. "You ladies wanna get a drink with me in there instead of out in this ghetto club? It's *dope* in'nere."

"Katie! Doesn't that sound cool?" I said, my voice ringing a little louder than I meant it to. "The VIP room!" I leapt up and down.

Katie looked at me crazily and murmured out of the side of her mouth, "Couldn't that be dangerous? And what about what's his name?"

"Who's what's his name?" Teddy asked.

We all looked over to the boys. Oh. Yes. Mike. I giggled. Suddenly everything seemed funny. Katie's lip gloss, for instance. The song that was playing through the speakers. I kept giggling. I knew I was drunk. But I couldn't control myself.

Katie's shoulders moved up and down, her hips shifting back and forth in frustration. "Heaven," she started. "You're really drunk."

"I am not," I said, feeling quite energized. "I'm perfectly fine."

"What's the deal with what's his name?" Teddy said again.

"Mike is his name," Katie said, "and he and Heaven were having an intimate conversation."

I started laughing uncontrollably.

"Is that right?" Teddy said, looking at me. "Well, who's he, anyway?" He puffed up his chest, brought his sunglasses down over his eyes, moved a little closer to me.

Oh my God. Was Teddy jealous?

The DJ switched to a slower song. A rush of people moved by us to get to the bar. I glanced at Steve and Mike. They were talking quietly, probably trying to figure out what to do. Was Teddy really so scary looking that they were just staying away completely? Whatever happened to friendly male competition?

"Come on, Kelly," Teddy said, changing the subject, trying to take Katie's arm. "Let's hit the VIP room. The VIP room is *smokin'*."

"It's Katie, not Kelly," Katie said, crossing her arms over her chest. "I think we should stay away from him," she said loudly, this time so Teddy could hear.

"Look, if you know what's good for you, you'll come with me to the vip room," Teddy said, saying "vip" instead of spelling it out. "They've got Cristal in there . . . and Courvoisier . . . *I'm* in there . . ."

"So?" Katie said. Teddy put a hand on the small of her back. She jumped away. "Don't touch me!" she shrieked.

"Katie, calm down," I said. "This isn't a big deal. Teddy's an old friend. Honest."

"Heaven, what are you *talking* about?" Katie said. "He's . . . You said he's part of . . ."

"Come on," I said, gritting my teeth. I knew what Katie was getting at. The yakuza.

"Is there a problem?" Steve stepped forward, trying to look tough. Although he looked pretty pathetic, really. He came up to Teddy's chest. I hadn't realized how tall Teddy was before. *That* made me laugh, too.

"No trouble, bro," Teddy said suavely, barely breaking a sweat. All he had to do was step forward a little and Steve backed off. "I got it in check, yo. Y'all are dismissed."

"Huh?" Mike said. I looked at him apologetically. Although in the light, he really wasn't so cute.

"Ya know, like the MTV show? *Dismissed*? Word," Teddy said.

"What?" Katie asked.

"Listen," Steve said, mustering up some courage from somewhere. "I'd watch it if I were you."

"Oh, yeah?" Teddy said, then put his hand on something under his coat. "Oh, yeah?" he said again.

The boys backed up.

"Dude, I thought they had metal detectors in here," Mike said.

"Heaven . . . ," Katie protested, looking nervously from me to Teddy.

"Not me," Teddy said. "I got in the back way. 'Cause these are my peeps."

My head spun. Teddy wasn't dumb enough to pull a gun in a crowded club. Right? I covered my mouth to conceal another giggle. I really had to stop this. I suddenly started to hiccup.

Katie stared at us all, horrified.

"Look," I said to Katie. "Let's just go for a little bit. For a drink. For half a drink. Then we can come back and find Steve and Mike or whoever. Or we can just dance. Whatever."

Katie looked at me like I'd lost my mind. The boys, by this point, had drifted away.

"Fine," she said at last. She looked pained. "Fine. But look, I don't think this is a good idea. If anything gets weird, seriously, Heaven, if you're coming back to my house, we have to get out of there. Quick." She bit her lip. "I want you safe, but I have to look out for me, too. I don't want to be involved in any of this again."

"No, no, I totally get it," I said. "I don't want this to be a . . . danger to you. We'll talk to him for just a couple of minutes." If I had been in a more sober mind-set, perhaps I would have been more timid about walking into the VIP room of a club with Teddy Yukemura.

And I knew that if I didn't follow Teddy and hang out with him for just a little bit, he might get mad enough to report back to his father and . . . something might happen. I could get myself into the same kind of troubles with the Yukemuras all over again. So I had to play it cool.

I wanted to explain this to Katie, but there was no time. Teddy swept us into the VIP room. Katie scowled. "Come on," I whispered to her. "It'll be okay. Just one drink."

To my relief, there were other people in the VIP room. Teddy had been telling the truth – it was an honest-to-God VIP room and not some weird Yukemura hangout. Normal-looking people stood all around us, laughing, drinking, smoking. Most of them looked totally smashed. One guy tumbled off his bar stool, and his date bent over, laughing, not even helping him up.

Teddy walked in front of us. When we hit the inside of the room, he quickly strolled up to two well-dressed Latino guys sitting at the bar. They both had slicked-back hair and impeccable suits and were smoking skinny cigars. They swayed on their stools, quite drunk. He bent his head down, looked shiftily back and forth, and put on this weird, ass-kissy, fake smile, as if he was trying to appease them. They stared at him coolly, not saying anything back. One of them stared directly at me. He didn't blink.

Something about them seemed shady. Katie tensed up.

Teddy called us over. "This is Pablo and Diego," he said. Up close, the guys were just as smooth as Teddy. Diego even kissed Katie's hand. Katie looked a little nervous. "Hi," she said back, trying to smile. I smiled at her sweetly. "We'll get out of here soon," I murmured.

Pablo and Diego turned to me. Diego did the same hand kiss, but Pablo was still staring at me intensely. One eyebrow was raised. He was staring unashamedly. He was making me blush. "What?" I said finally.

He looked away. "Nothing," he said. "Forgive me. You are very beautiful. That's all." He gave Diego a look. Teddy tried to signal the bartender.

"So listen," I said to Teddy in a low voice so the weird dudes he was with couldn't hear. "Were you in L.A. a couple of weeks ago, at a club? I thought I saw you . . ."

Teddy shook his head. "I split out of L.A."

"But how? And what happened to you? And why did you help me?"

"Hold up there," Teddy said. "I split out of L.A. One of my peeps helped me. I'm hidin' out from my pops for a while, but I'll be goin' back eventually. I have to patch things up, but we both need a little time to cool off."

"Your pops and his goons tried to kidnap me again," I said sullenly.

"Are you sure?" Teddy asked, his voice edgy.

"I looked right at him," I said. "It was one of the guys from the garage."

Teddy grunted. "Yo, I knew nothing about that," he said. "I didn't know they were going to try to do that. I've been in Vegas for a couple of weeks now."

I thought I'd seen Teddy at Vibe. Was he telling me the truth, or had he been in Vegas for only a few days? Could he have seen me at Vibe and tipped off his father's henchmen that I was in the club? Would Teddy do that? No. I had to believe him.

We were quiet for a minute. "Listen, thanks . . . ," I said. "I mean . . . I don't know why you decided to give me the information on where the kidnappers would be, but I really appreciate it . . ."

Teddy started waving his arms around. "Heaven, no worries. Don't even sweat it," he said. Then he signalled the bartender. "Dewar's, rocks," he said. He looked at me. "What do you want?"

"Cosmo," I said. "But you know, I was worried about you after that."

"Word?" Teddy asked, grinning. "You were worried about me?"

"Well, I mean . . ." I trailed off. "Yeah, I was. You looked out for someone other than yourself, and I know you needed the money, and I'm sure your father was really upset . . ."

"Naw, they were holding me for a while, you know. No biggie. Then my boy busted me out."

Teddy was looking in the other direction when I saw the scars on his arm. They were black, about the size of a dime. Six each. Had someone put out burning cigarettes on his arm? Were they *torturing* him? Would his own father torture Teddy? I felt a little woozy. My eyes darted over to Pablo and Diego. They were talking intensely. Both were chain-smoking brown cigarettes.

"I had to get outta town, lemme tell you that," Teddy continued. Then he looked off into space.

"Are you going to go back? What are you going to do?"

"I have a couple of deals working in other places," Teddy said cryptically.

"Yo, T.," Pablo said. "I got a call from Raphael earlier about the craps table. He lookin' to collect."

"I already gave him what I owed," Teddy said gruffly. I stood there, waiting. Teddy's tongue lolled out of his mouth. He seemed pretty drunk.

"No, no, you didn't," said Diego, wavering, nearly falling off the stool. "You did the hard eight a coupla times and then you crapped out and lost all yo' chips."

"What the hell are you talking about, bruthuh?" Teddy said, slurring his words.

"The hard eight is harder than the easy eight," Pablo mumbled. "Those dice are loco."

Diego started to laugh.

"I don't owe nobody money!" Teddy said gruffly.

"I'm not even talking about the big money, T. You wanna get into that now, d'jou?"

Katie and I stood in the corner quietly, watching the conversation continue. "Let's get out of here," Katie said. "This doesn't look good." Who were these guys? What was this money Teddy owed? Did he have a gambling problem?

The clock was nearing 4 a.m. Katie glanced at the angry Diego and Pablo again. They glowered at Teddy. Teddy scowled back. I worried: Were they the types of guys who were totally aggressive and angry when they got drunk, like the tormenting crowd in *8 Mile*? Or like those guys in *Fight Club*? I thought about a bar brawl, complete with Teddy's gun, and shivered.

"Sounds like a plan," I said. I hadn't really talked with Teddy about what I'd wanted to talk about – namely, why, exactly, he'd saved me from being kidnapped and what had happened to him afterwards – but I was dead tired, too. I tapped Teddy on the shoulder, breaking him away from his argument. He looked up, stunned. Apparently he'd been falling asleep midargument.

"We're gonna go," I said.

"No, don't go!" Teddy said. "Seriously, stay a little longer." I couldn't quite make out what he was saying. To me, it sounded like *"stahhalugger."* That Dewar's on the rocks must have hit him hard.

"No, we're tired, seriously," I said.

"Well, then lemme drive you," Teddy said, leaning down and half falling off the stool. "We need to talk more."

"I'm sure I'll see you again," I said vaguely. I didn't know how to leave it with Teddy. I half trusted him. I knew he wasn't 100 per cent good, but he *was* looking out for me. And besides Katie, he was the only person in this world who seemed to want me around.

"Yeah, we're cool," Katie said, a little impatiently. "We'll get a cab."

We exited quickly, saying a brief goodbye to Pablo and Diego. Pablo took my hand and kissed it. "You are just so beautiful," he said in a thick Spanish accent. "What is your name again?"

I didn't answer. Teddy blurted, "*Isn't* she beautiful? Didn't I tell you before? Her name's Heaven."

"Heaven, ah?" he said. "It is nice to meet you, Miss Heaven." He squeezed my hand a little hard. I winced, feeling pretty creeped out. There was *something* wrong. Then he stood up and walked back in the direction of the bathrooms.

We stepped out under the dark sky. The neon was still flashing everywhere; people were still wandering around. Cars were still zooming up the Strip.

"God, that was interesting," Katie said.

As soon as I sat down in the cab, my head really started

to spin. I'd probably had – four drinks? Five? "I might be sick," I said. My stomach lurched.

"Really? Oh God, Heaven, do we need to pull over?"

The nausea passed quickly. "I think I'm all right," I said after a minute. "I'm sorry about Teddy. But he's really okay, you know."

"But Heaven, he's *not*," Katie said. "Remember how awful he was the first time you met him? And he's part of the yakuza, for God's sake!"

"So's my father," I snapped.

"Well . . ." Katie trailed off. I'd caught her off guard. "But now you're all like . . . buddy-buddy with him? Heaven, he was carrying a *gun*."

"Yeah, yeah," I said blearily. "He's all talk but no action."

"And he's *such* a druggie. It's obvious those guys he was hanging out with were drug dealers. It's obvious they were all on something the whole night."

"Oh, you don't know those things for sure," I said, although I suspected Katie was totally right.

"It seemed so *obvious*," Katie said. "He's totally not going to live past twenty-five. He seems involved in such dangerous stuff, Heaven. You really shouldn't be talking to him. He's . . . scary."

"Believe me, Teddy's not scary," I said, impatience rising in my voice. I knew he was dangerous. I also knew that it was pretty stupid that we'd hung out with him at all. But I felt defensive all of a sudden. Teddy *had* helped me once. I had to give him *some* credit. "I kidnapped him on a bus once," I said. "I flipped him over my shoulder once. Teddy is . . . Teddy is a teddy *bear*."

"Heaven, you're so drunk," Katie said. Then she burst out laughing. "I doubt you could flip him over your shoulder!"

I felt the urge to explain to Katie all the training I'd done and that I definitely *could* flip Teddy over my shoulder and that I *had*, on the streets of L.A., and that he wasn't really a gorilla at all but a bit more complex than that. But before I could, the cab pulled up to what I supposed was Katie's apartment, somewhere in the outskirts of Vegas. I rolled out of the cab, giggling. "The Katie palace," I said. "Gambling until dawn!"

The alcohol sloshed in my stomach. I turned my head to see why Katie wasn't laughing. And then I heard her scream. All my senses rushed back to me. I whipped my body around to see what had happened.

Six men surrounded us, cloaked in black ninja robes. They moved right for me silently, their arms poised for battle.

I call up my jefe in Tijuana. "I've talked to him," I say. "But I don't know if he wants to come up with the money. He won't budge."

"We've waited too long!" he snarls back at me. "He's making a fool out of us!"

I fold my phone shut and pace back and forth. I can hear loud talking back in the VIP room. He's brought two girls with him – but the one, que linda. Gorgeous. She looks familiar. I have a feeling I know who she is. I haven't known this Teddy for long, but I can guess that he brings around these different model-type girls often. Perhaps because of his father. Because of his largeness, his confidence. The way he throws money around. Although this girl is different.

I'm not sure if I can trust this Teddy. Does he know what he's doing? Why have we had to follow him out here to Vegas from L.A.? Apparently he had to leave there suddenly. Why?

I go into the bathroom and stare at myself in the mirror. Make sure my hair is in its proper place. But this bar has no beautiful women, really. Except for this Heaven. But Teddy says she belongs to him. Perhaps if she is not with him that way . . . perhaps . . . since he knows our deal . . . perhaps we could work something out. I would like to have a few hours with this girl on my own. I would show her that Japanese men have nothing on the Colombians. Teddy comes messily into the bathroom, practically falling over.

"Hola," *I say as he staggers over to the urinals.*

"Ho," Teddy says, barely getting out the first syllable. Finally he sputters out the second: "La." When I drink too much, I get angry, violent. Everything I can't control comes forth in a barrage of punches. Teddy falls apart, becomes a wrecked house of cards.

How can I trust a house of cards?

Teddy straightens up from the urinal and comes over, without washing his hands, to inspect himself in the mirror. He lays a hand on me.

"I'm glads yous and Diegos decided to meet me tonight," he slurs. *"I knew you'd see things going my way seeing."*

I look at his reflection in the mirror. "Who's the girl?" I ask, although I know the answer.

He grins, straightening up. He crosses his arms over his chest smugly.

"She's my fiancée." He uncrosses his arms and lights a cigarette, still smiling. "Pretty hot, huh?" Then he turns and shoves out the door with his shoulder.

Pablo

6

The ninjas quivered, waving their shogei knives gracefully in the air.

Katie let out another mind-numbing scream.

I sprang into action, whirled around, and kicked the one closest to Katie. He didn't have time to react and fell quickly. I grabbed Katie and rushed her to the bushes, practically pushing her in. Katie yelped in fear.

"Stay there," I commanded. She looked up at me with confused and terrified eyes. I didn't have time to dwell on it. The ninjas moved closer to me.

I prowled around a little, keeping them all at a distance. When one got close enough to strike me, I was able to defend myself with a series of blocks and rolls. I tried my shinobi-iri technique, but it didn't quite work here – there were no shadows to slide into. One of the ninjas was able to kick me in the jaw. I bit my tongue and tasted blood. My jaw went numb with pain. Tears sprang to my eyes.

"*Shikkan,*" one of them growled. Surrender.

I managed to hold them off for a little longer with a series of kicks, but I could feel panic creeping in. I gathered up every ounce of strength I had. If I didn't, something might happen to Katie.

One of the ninjas kicked me in the gut and I flailed backwards. The blow made all the contents of my stomach – the long forgotten burger, the cosmopolitans – rise up. I coughed and looked at what I'd spit out on my hand. Blood.

Another ninja rushed towards me. I could see only his cold, soulless eyes. But I couldn't think of a defense. A bizarre mishmash of images gathered together in my head: the blinking lights of the Sahara casino, the taste of Mike's mouth when he'd kissed me, the smell of Teddy's breath – rank and alcoholic. The glint of Pablo's smile, the silver of Diego's watch. Hiro, standing alone as he watched me climb aboard the bus.

I was losing this battle.

I dodged a ninja's kick to my chest by ducking and rolling. The grass felt wet and sticky. Was it dew or my blood? I managed to do a takedown move on one of the ninjas from the ground, but the strength I had to muster from my quadriceps drew all the life out of me. He fell in a pile on top of me, and I couldn't shrug him off.

"Heaven!" Katie screamed from the bushes.

Hearing her voice forced me to stand up, but the ninjas were close. As soon as I stood up completely, my head started to spin. I backed away but realized I was backing into the wall of Katie's building – something Hiro had told me time and again never to do. "Don't back into a wall or an alley or a corner," he'd said. "You don't want to be kyuuchou – a cornered bird. Don't let your enemy drive you to that."

I looked around desperately. I had backed into a little alcove in the front of the building. The grass was even wetter back here – I could feel it on my ankles. A sprinkler sprayed the grass and brushed against my leg. I quivered.

"Shit," I whispered.

Suddenly a cracking noise erupted in the sky. Everyone ducked. A gunshot. I took a risk while the ninjas were guarding themselves: I leapt over them, rushed into the open space. I kept my head covered, kept checking my back.

Who was shooting?

The ninjas froze. I froze. They were inches away from me. I looked over and saw the whites of one of the ninja's eyes. He stared at me with a steely and menacing gaze.

A second shot sounded. My attackers ducked again.

A figure emerged from the bushes, pointing the gun at the group of ninjas around me. Or maybe the figure was pointing the gun at me. I trembled. *Oh my God,* I thought. *It's pointed at me. They've got guns now.*

I checked to hear Katie's breathing. I couldn't. Had they shot her? Oh God, no . . .

Suddenly the figure stepped into the porch light. And then I saw.

Teddy.

He held the gun steadily, still pointing it at the ninjas. His hand didn't quiver at all – he certainly didn't seem as drunk as he had before. He glared at the group of ninjas. I still shivered, standing in the centre. No one spoke.

Teddy shook the gun a little, pointing it one by one at each ninja. They didn't flinch, but they didn't continue to attack me, either.

"Hikisanasai!" Teddy growled. *Leave.* He waved his gun around the circle. The ninjas backed away, afraid of what the gun could do. Slips in the air, they vanished in seconds.

When I was no longer surrounded, I looked up at Teddy, who was still standing at a distance, watching them go. He seemed so levelheaded. But at the bar . . . hadn't he been totally loaded? How had he sobered up so quickly? How had he known to follow us home?

Teddy rushed up to me. Katie rolled out of the bushes, crying.

"We've got to get out of here," he said hurriedly.

"What's going on?" I demanded. "I thought I'd be safe

here. Who were they? Did they have something to do with those Latino guys at the bar?"

Teddy shook his head. "Come on. We've got to get you out of Vegas."

"What do you mean, not safe?" Katie wailed, her first words since the attack had begun.

"I don't know who they were," Teddy said, answering my earlier question. "But I know that it's not safe. That I can explain to you. And that's all I can explain."

"What do you mean?" Katie said again, hysterical.

I still felt drunk and horrible. And beat up. But Teddy seemed even, calm. I'd never seen him this levelheaded, calm and brave. At our wedding he'd been a scared little baby. Was he *on* something? Perhaps something to . . . speed him up? Slow him down? I didn't even know what sort of drug he'd need. But then I thought of something even more interesting: Maybe at the bar, he'd been pretending.

"What's going on?" Katie asked again, clearly crazed that no one was answering her question.

"Heaven and I have got to leave Vegas," Teddy said evenly. "Things aren't safe here for us."

Katie whimpered, her eyes wide. "Heaven, you told me that you weren't safe, you told me that these things were happening to you, and I saw your eye and everything, but . . . I didn't know . . ."

Tears started running down her face. I ran my hand over

the bottom of my jaw. It felt tender. I was going to have a big bruise.

"Knowing it and seeing it are two different things," Teddy said, finishing her thought. He finally put his gun back into his waistband of his trousers. "Come on. Let's go inside and make a plan."

7

How had they found me?

"Keep the lights off," Teddy said. "We don't want to draw attention to ourselves."

"This apartment looks out onto a courtyard," Katie said angrily. "Not the front of the building. Who would see us?" She glared at Teddy, then lit a bunch of candles. "I'll make coffee," she said in a dead voice.

Once it was ready, Katie handed me a cup of coffee and we sat down on the couch. I drank it but felt even dizzier. "Ugh," I said. I had completely botched the fight. My limbs had moved sluggishly. My mind had been clogged with useless stuff. I hadn't used any of the tactics Hiro had taught me.

"Vegas isn't safe for either of us," Teddy announced. "That attack proved it."

"But wait," I said. "Were they attacking you or me? If I hadn't spoken to you, would this have happened to me?"

"I don't know," Teddy said, a little exasperated. "Why do you think I'd know?"

"It just . . . it just seems that every time I run into *you*, I get attacked by ninjas!" I said. But then I thought about it. Those ninjas had descended on me like dogs realizing where the really *good* meat was. The steak. They obviously knew I was the target, the prize. I clamped my mouth shut.

But Teddy was keyed up. "I think we should get out of here," he said again. "We should leave Vegas ASAP. We both should. Together."

"I don't think we should have to *leave*," I said. "I mean, yeah, this house is probably marked now . . . but couldn't we, like, go to a hotel or something?"

Katie sighed. It made me feel worse – I'd come here and promised Katie that she wouldn't be involved in any of the past bad stuff that had happened in my life – that we were completely free of danger. But I'd been wrong.

Teddy shook his head. "No hotels," he said. "It doesn't make sense. We have to get out of here. Tonight." He said it with such chilling forcefulness that I felt like we were in danger if we stayed here, in Katie's apartment, for another *minute*.

"Heaven," Katie said in a small voice, "I think he's right. I think you should go somewhere that's safer. Wherever that might be. Although I don't know if you should go with him." She pointed at Teddy. "You could have been killed out there. I saw what they were doing to you. Is this what's been happening?" She played with a tassel on one of her pillows.

"Pretty much," I said, bringing my hand up to my bruised eye.

Katie looked ghostly in the candlelight. "I didn't really think that this . . . was what would happen to you . . . because of who Konishi is," she said softly.

"Who knows if this even has to do with Konishi," I said.

Teddy grunted. Katie didn't say anything. I could see a large tear on her cheek.

"So," Katie went on, "I think you should leave, but I don't think you should leave with . . . him."

"You said that already," Teddy said. "She's got to leave with me. I'm her ticket out of here."

"What are you talking about? Why are *you* her ticket out of here?" Katie said obstinately. "There has to be another solution. We should call Hiro." I heard her get up, walk over to where I guessed her phone was. "What's his number?"

I perked up despite myself. Hiro! Could this be a way to reach out to him? If someone *else* called him? Or would he answer, hear the name *Heaven*, and immediately hang up?

"No way," Teddy said. "That's a stupid idea. Hiro was just this guy who put you up for a little while. Whatever." He waved his hand to the side. "Why would we call him? What's he gonna do about it? Why does he have anything to do with any of this? This isn't Hiro's problem." He said "Hiro" the way one would say "tumorous mass".

"He's more than just some guy I stayed with when I got here," I said. "He was a friend of Ohiko's."

Teddy grunted. When he'd been trying to find me in L.A., he'd attacked Hiro while he was working at his bike messenger job. Apparently he'd pinned Hiro to the ground for a few moments and demanded to know what Hiro was doing with me and whether it was romantic or not. Then Hiro had flipped him and told him to buzz off.

"Let's not get him involved," Teddy said gruffly.

I had a feeling Teddy was a little jealous of Hiro. But what he said was true. This wasn't Hiro's problem. And how would Katie explain it on the phone? *It's 5 a.m., please come rescue Heaven 'cause she's in trouble? She sucks 'cause she can't even last a day in Vegas without you?* I mean, maybe if she mentioned Teddy's name and ninjas . . .

But Hiro would probably say what Teddy just did. *This is her problem. She has to solve it for herself. I've told her to strike out on her own. She has to forget me.*

I wasn't ready to hear it again.

Teddy walked towards the door. "We've got to go *now*," he said to me. "Come on. Before something else happens."

Katie followed him. "I still don't think it's a good idea," she said, her voice shaking. "Look, I don't know what the hell is going on. But I just don't have a good feeling about this."

"Dude, I saved your life," Teddy said gruffly. "Does that count for anything?"

"Yes, I realize that," Katie said in sort of a teacherly voice – the tone she used when she was trying to explain English grammar to me. "But how do we know that it isn't really *you* who's behind the attacks?" She pointed at Teddy and frowned. "Why did you know to follow us home, after all?"

Teddy snorted. "That's the dumbest thing I've ever heard. I was just looking out for Heaven."

Katie stomped her foot in frustration. "Look, jackass, I have a long history with her, too! You can't just take her like this! There's something more to you than you're letting on, and I don't think this is right! I think that attack was something of your doing! We would've been fine if we hadn't run into you!" After she finished her mini-tirade, she slumped back on the couch and put her head in her hands. I could tell she was crying because her shoulders were shaking.

"Katie . . . ," I said softly. "I think Teddy's right. I think I'm going to have to go with him. It's the safest thing to do right now. Believe me, if I didn't think it was a good idea, I wouldn't be going." I didn't quite believe this myself, but I had to comfort Katie somehow. Although the idea of moving filled my body with utter dread. I would have to be on the run again. With Teddy. He still scared me a little.

"All right, let's quit standing around, yo," Teddy said. "Let's bust a move."

I stood back up and grabbed my coat and bag, a new wave of anger washing over me. Katie and Teddy glared at each other from opposite sides of the room.

I picked up my bag and walked to the door with Teddy.

"Call the cops," Teddy said to Katie. "Say that you were attacked outside your apartment and you feel really scared right now. They'll probably be of some help. And watch your back for the next couple of days. But really, once they realize we've split, they won't want anything to do with you. It's us they've been looking for."

"Okay," Katie said shakily. We stood in the doorway. The sun was starting to peek over the horizon. "Well," she said to me, "be safe."

"Yeah," I said. I couldn't bring any emotion into my voice. If I let anything in, it would flood uncontrollably – I'd probably start crying. So I had to stay stoic, blank. "I'll try," I said. "You too."

Katie looked quickly at Teddy and then back at me again, as if to give me a signal with her eyes. Her lip quivered. I could tell she was thinking that associating with Teddy meant certain death for me, too.

We clomped down the stairs and into Teddy's car. It was a BMW with plush leather seats. I sat down rigidly, looking up at the apartment complex, trying to figure out which window was Katie's. What if Katie was right? Was if this *was* certain death for me?

What if I'd made the wrong choice?

Gojo comes into my office and lingers in front of my desk. I type on my computer for a good three or four minutes until the silence becomes unbearable.

"What?" I snap.

"Someone has seen your son," he says. "I just got a call."

"Why didn't you say so?" I say. "Where?"

My son has escaped. Someone must have let him out. Could it be this drug connection he has? Could it be because of Heaven Kogo? In any case, he is disloyal. Kaoyogoshi, a disgrace. He should commit seppuku if he has any morals at all.

But he also cannot be trusted. He is a planner. He wants something of his own.

"Las Vegas," Gojo says. "One of your contacts there in the New York, New York casino recognized him. He was walking down the street with two other men. Looked Latino."

Why didn't Gojo give me this call instead of fielding it himself? Rage runs through me. It sounds like he was walking with the Colombians. Those akuma men. Devils. Loyal to no one. Greedy. My son is greedy as well. All greedy akuma.

"Should we send for someone to get him?" Gojo asks.

"It is you who should go," I say bitterly, "since you are the one who let him escape in the first place."

Gojo recoils. "I wasn't!" he says quickly.

I look at him suspiciously. "No?" I ask. "Are you sure?"
Gojo doesn't look me in the eye.

"Who let him go?" I bark.

"I don't know," he says quietly. "But I think he needs to come back to you. You have to make this right."

I turn back to my computer in rage. "Send someone out there to get him," I say. "But not in anger. Do not have someone throw him into the back of a car but instead offer the olive branch. Just say I would like to forgive and make peace with him."

Gojo nods and stands there, as if he is going to say something.

"What?" I scream.

He jumps. "Nothing," he says, and turns to leave.

Takeda will come back, thinking he is in my good graces once again. And then, like a waiting tiger, I will strike.

Yuji

8

As the sun began to send orange and purple streaks through the morning sky, Teddy and I drove out of Vegas. The only sound was the air whistling through the open windows.

About half an hour in I noticed that the road signs were telling us that we were driving towards L.A. "All right, stop the car," I said.

"What?" Teddy said.

"Are you insane?" I shrieked. "Are you driving us back to L.A?"

"Yes," Teddy said. "My dogs can help us."

"Are you completely *brain damaged*?" I said. "We both had to flee L.A. Did I tell you that someone burned down the place where I was staying? Did I tell you that I have nowhere to go in L.A? Did I tell you that if I had known this was where we were going, I wouldn't have got in the car with you?"

"Look, don't freak," Teddy said. "I promise you you're gonna be safe. And anyway, Vegas is lame. I'm glad to be outta there."

"But we can't go to L.A.!" I said again, panicking. "There's no one I can trust there!" I thought fleetingly of Hiro. "Turn the car around. Let's go back to Vegas. We can hide in a hotel and think."

"No can do," Teddy said. "I'm over the whole Vegas scene. I had to split."

I read between the lines. Teddy *couldn't* go back to Vegas. He probably *did* have massive gambling debts. Maybe something even worse than that.

Rage bubbled up inside me. So the attack in front of Katie's house had really had everything to do with Teddy?

But wait. They wanted *me*. They'd followed *me*.

But Teddy seemed to think the attack had something to do with him.

But then . . . he'd scared them away with his gun.

God, I was confused.

What was I doing in this car?

"So, what, have you pissed off Diego and Pablo or something?" I asked. "Are they drug dealers?"

"No," Teddy said, too quickly. He was lying. There was fear in his voice.

We sped along the straight highway, headed towards L.A.

"Listen, I really think L.A. is the best for us right now. We can lay low in this place my buddy's got, figure out what's what, then maybe get out of the country," he said.

"Haven't you heard me at all?" I said, my voice rising to a higher pitch. "I think this is a bad idea." Then something horrible occurred to me. "Is this . . . is this just some plot to marry me again?"

"Well," Teddy said. My heart pounded. Oh my God. This *was* what he was planning. Oh God, get me out of this car! "If you think about it, marrying would solve everything. It could buy us some time."

"No!" I shrieked. I clutched the door handle. "God, I *knew* you were too good to be true! Like, you'd got all like good-hearted and everything, and maybe you had a little moment of weakness or morality or whatever when you got me out of the marriage a couple of weeks ago, but obviously that was just temporary insanity, is that it?"

"No . . . ," Teddy said.

I kept going. "You haven't changed one bit, Teddy. You're still bugging me about the same stuff! 'Buy us some time'? What does that even mean? How would that buy us some time?" I sighed.

"Look, we won't have to act all husband and wife and shit," Teddy said. "And I didn't give you the 411 on that kidnapping for my own good – I did it for you. But Heaven . . . this is really the way out for us. Otherwise we'll just be on the run . . . until they find us."

"Oh my God, you are *so* frustrating!" I said, screwing my

eyes up in rage. "Do you know something that I don't? Do you know who is looking for me?"

"No!" Teddy said. "All I'm saying is, if we got married, I'd be in good with my dad again, and he'd give us a lot of Yukemura protection. Nothing could hurt us."

"Great," I said. "That's really comforting. *Yukemura protection*. I've heard that I can get Kogo protection, too. It sounds very reassuring."

"It really wouldn't be that bad. I could try to make it as comfortable for you as possible. You're my girl, Heaven. I'm lookin' out for you."

I balled up my fists. I never, *ever* wanted to be a yakuza wife. No way. Especially a wife connected to the Yukemura family – thieves, pimps, drug runners, embezzlers, killers.

"I'm sorry," I said. "I still can't agree to it."

"But I've proved my loyalty to you, Heaven," Teddy said. "Yo, this isn't for the cash! This is for something more!"

"Oh, that's not a *tiny* little bit of why you're suggesting this?" I said angrily.

Teddy didn't say anything.

I sighed loudly and searched through my bag for an aspirin. "Please. If you really care about me, drive me anywhere but L.A. Honestly. Can you please do this for me?"

Teddy didn't say anything for a long time. The road signs for L.A. were coming faster – it looked like we were only about an hour away now. Plus the clock said almost nine – peak rush hour. The traffic had slowed down. I swerved my head around to see if we were being tailed. In the daylight Teddy's BMW would be easy to spot.

"Okay. I got an idea. Why don't we go to Joshua Tree?" Teddy said finally. "It seems totally remote. We could check into a hotel."

"Joshua Tree?" I asked. Wasn't that the name of a U2 album?

"It's this totally dope park near Palm Springs," Teddy said. "It's far enough away from L.A. and it's mad private. I heard Beyonce and her crew went there like two weeks ago. We could max and relax, you know? I honestly don't think anyone's going to be searching for us at Joshua Tree. It's too romantic for anyone to guess."

I was quiet for a moment. If the place was anything like the U2 record, it would be paradise. Katie and I used to listen to the album relentlessly – especially "Bullet the Blue Sky" and "With or Without You". We listened to it as much as we listened to Dave Matthews's *Crash* and the second Coldplay CD, *A Rush of Blood to the Head*.

Maybe if we went to Joshua Tree, I could figure out a foolproof way to get the hell out of here.

"All right," I said. "Let's go. Do you know how to get there?"

"Yeah!" Teddy said. "It can't be too hard. I mean, I've seen a ton of road signs for it." He seemed positively ecstatic. "Really?" he said. "You'll really go?"

"Yeah," I said. "It sounds better than L.A."

"Wicked," Teddy said, smiling. I smiled, too, weakly.

We drove up to a hotel outside the red, rocky entrance. From the outside, the park looked gorgeous. The hotel sign said Eden Hotel. A smaller sign said This Way to the Spa.

Spa. That was a word I hadn't heard in a long time.

I sat on one of the lobby's large leather sofas while Teddy asked about room availability. He walked back to me, grinning, holding a key. "We're in luck!" he said. "They had a room. A cancellation."

"Great," I said. I looked around the lobby. It was like a beautiful lodge – all woodsy and warm, with brightly patterned pottery and blankets. The air had a bit of a chill to it; there was a fire in the corner.

"So . . . you want to go for a drive or what? See the park?" Teddy asked.

I looked down at myself. What I really wanted were some new clothes and a bath. I was still wearing the ridiculous tube top Katie had given me for the club. I didn't even have the shirt I'd worn on the bus to Vegas – Katie had put it in her bag, and we'd forgotten it in the rush to leave. I frowned. Katie had promised to lend me some clothes. We'd forgotten to do that, too.

I spied a sign saying Boutique and an arrow. At the very least, I needed something more normal to sleep in, especially if I was going to be in the same room as Teddy. "I'm going to just go into this shop for a minute," I said. "But then, fine. Let's look at the park."

"Sure, okay. Whatever," Teddy said. He was being very conciliatory, probably because I'd agreed to come to Joshua Tree with him. He probably couldn't believe it. *She's going along with my plan*, I imagined him thinking.

Oh, maybe I was just being paranoid. Maybe Teddy wasn't that sinister and sneaky. But why else would he be so psyched that I was in this hotel with him?

Unless . . .

I walked into the boutique. I bought a T-shirt for sleeping and underwear but then realized I was much lower on cash than I'd thought. I didn't want to blow all my money on clothes if I'd have to escape. Great. I'd have to spend the next who knew how long in this slinky tube top.

Teddy raised his eyebrows provocatively at the sight of my new underwear through the clear shopping bag (totally nonsexy stuff: basic white cotton underwear) and led me back to the car. I was dying to see what the park looked like. He gunned the engine and we rolled slowly to the entrance.

"It's ten dollars to get in," the woman at a little kiosk at the gate told us. Darn. I reached for my wallet – another expense I hadn't thought of – but Teddy stopped me. "I'll get this," he said, shelling out a twenty.

"Thanks," I mumbled. We drove on.

The park was beautiful. The day had passed quickly, and the sun was dropping as we were driving in. The rocks were this gorgeous purple hue and the cactuses made arresting silhouettes in the sky. I couldn't even compare it to any movie or thing on TV I'd seen before. All I could think of was *Joshua Tree*, the U2 album, running in a constant loop over and over and over again in my head. Come to think of it, Katie and I had listened to *Joshua Tree* the day I'd found out I was to marry Teddy.

What a day that had been. My father had told me curtly over lunch. He'd taken time out of his busy schedule to have some sashimi with me, alone. Well, wait. Mieko was there. That's right. She sat quietly next to us, daintily eating her miso soup (she never ate much more than miso soup), not making a single sound. And my father said to me, completely deadpan: "We have found a match for you."

He explained who Teddy Yukemura was: a businessman from L.A. "A businessman?" I asked. "You *can't* be serious."

"I do not appreciate your disobedience," Konishi said. "This is a good match for you. He is a member of the Yukemura family."

That name sounded familiar, but I didn't know why. "Do you have a picture of him?" I asked. My father shook his head.

"He will be coming to Tokyo in a week's time to meet you." At that, he made a motion to get up from the table. Mieko sat there, her hands clasped together, a smug, infuriating smile on her face.

Had there been talk then that the marriage was a "business decision"? I couldn't remember. Of course, maybe if I'd listened a little closer, perhaps I would have picked up that my father and the Yukemuras had struck a deal to marry me off. The thought of that was even more chilling than the idea my father was simply sticking to traditional Japanese ways.

"Does Ohiko know?" I asked my father as he stood up to leave.

"I have just told him," he said, smoothing down his expensive suit. "But you must not disturb him. He is training with his sensei right now."

"Isn't this kind of important?" I demanded. "Why isn't Ohiko sitting with us, discussing this, too?"

"This does not concern your brother," my father answered sharply, and left.

The next day, Ohiko was gone. And then the next time I saw him was the last day of his life.

I'd fled upstairs and Katie and I had listened to fast, guitar-jangly stuff – The White Stripes, The Donnas, the Yeah Yeah Yeahs. I turned up the volume even though my father forbade it. I felt like smashing things.

Oh. And Mieko had said something strange at that lunch, too. She'd smiled and said, "Heaven, your life will be far better with Takeda."

She'd looked like she had something up her sleeve. If only I could go back and pay closer attention to Mieko.

There had been something so sinister and suspicious about her, but I couldn't quite figure out what.

"Isn't this beautiful?" Teddy said, jerking me back to the present. The sky had faded to a light lavender. The sun was sinking below the rocks.

As I looked at the scenery and thought about how much my life had changed, I began to feel a strange twinge. A twinge for Hiro. My love for him felt stronger than ever.

"It is beautiful." I sighed.

Teddy turned to me. "This could be really good for us. Don't you think we'd be a good couple?"

I didn't answer, pretending to be totally absorbed in the landscape. I couldn't just *marry* Teddy. That would be a betrayal to Hiro somehow.

But wait. He'd told me to *forget him*.

What if I called him? Didn't this qualify as danger? I was stuck in a car with Teddy Yukemura. There had been another attack on my life. So my mission was about forgetting him. Why couldn't I say I was *having trouble with my mission, please call to discuss?*

I didn't know why I hadn't thought of it before. Hiro had helped when I'd had trouble with other missions. That was what he was *there* for. He was my sensei.

Okay. I would call him later, when we got back to the hotel. But . . . but what if he was really serious about this mission? What if he wouldn't take my call?

I'd give him a time limit to call back. Forty-eight hours.

That seemed like enough time for him to think it over, then decide. Two days. I breathed in and out. If he didn't call me in two days, I'd know that I had to continue this struggle on my own.

The sky was completely dark now. "You want to get some eats?" Teddy asked me. "I think I saw a restaurant in the hotel."

We headed back to our little bungalow of a hotel room. Teddy opened the door. "Yo, yo, *yo!*" he said.

The room was amazing. It was candlelit, with large windows and a luxurious bed. All the colours were calming earth tones, and it smelled lovely. To the left, I could see a gigantic bathroom with an enormous tub.

"Wow," I echoed. I wondered how we would sort out the sleeping arrangements. "I'll sleep on the floor," Teddy said, reading my mind. "Or – you know what? There might be cots available downstairs. I can go check. I wanted to see the outside of this place, anyway. Apparently they've got a phat pool. You wanna come?"

"I think I'll lie down for a little bit," I said. "If you don't mind."

"C'mon, please?" Teddy said. "I bet it's the bomb."

"I can look at it later," I said. "I haven't slept . . ."

Teddy still hesitated. Then I realized: he thought I was going to escape. "Honestly, I'm just going to lie down," I said. "I'm not *going* anywhere. I promise."

"Okay," he said uncertainly. He still didn't move. I lay

down on the bed and put a pillow over my head. He stood there for a long time, then I finally heard the latch click and the door close.

I was alone.

I rooted through my bag to find my traceless cell phone. I didn't want to make this call on the hotel phone: the number would show up on the bill. Teddy might recognize it. My heart pounded as the phone rang. And rang. And rang.

"Hello?" Karen picked up.

Nerves streaked through my stomach. For some dumb reason, I hadn't thought of the possibility that Karen might answer. Shit. This girl hated me. She'd told me off on several different occasions. "Uh . . . Karen," I said. "It's Heaven."

"Oh."

There was a pause.

"How are you, Heaven?" she said softly.

"I'm . . . I'm fine," I said. I was taken aback by her sweet tone of voice. "Um . . . is Hiro there? I—"

"He isn't, I'm afraid," Karen interrupted. "Sorry about that."

Why was she being Superpolite Girl?

"Oh . . . well . . . can you give him a message?"

"Of course. Let me get a pen."

She got off the line. I was afraid she was going to hang up, but then she came back. "Okay, all ready," she said.

"I'm at Joshua Tree in bungalow number nine. Please tell

him I need him to meet me. Or at least call me back. He can call my cell phone. Here's the number." I gave her the digits.

"Joshua Tree. How nice," Karen murmured.

"Well . . . it's not like that, exactly. I'm with Teddy Yukemura." I didn't know if Karen knew who Teddy was, but maybe she'd write that down in the message.

"Uh-huh," Karen cooed. What, had she decided to take her medication today? I was completely confused. Or . . . or maybe she wanted to make amends.

She repeated my number back to me. "Is that right?" she said.

"Um, yeah," I said cautiously. "Tell him it's urgent."

"Of course," she said.

Okay. This was just too strange. But I figured . . . maybe we could patch things up. "Listen, Karen, I'm really sorry about everything," I started. "I've been wanting to explain to you and make things right, but now I'm out of town . . ."

"Oh, don't worry," Karen said. "It's really no problem, Heaven. I understand everything. Okay, I have to go now. I'll give Hiro the message. Bye!"

She hung up. I hit the end button and stared at my phone.

I hang up the phone.

What is she doing calling him?

Things have been tense between Hiro and me. I'm not the kind of girl who gets all worked up if the guy I'm interested in doesn't call me for a whole day or acts distant if we get into a fight about something. But this is different. There's something wrong.

Hiro hasn't been explaining a lot of things to me since our relationship began. I can accept this. There are some things that I just should not know, some things that are for him and Heaven to deal with. I realize who Heaven is and the danger she is in. When I remarked yesterday that I hadn't seen Heaven in a while and Hiro said that she had gone away, I will admit that I breathed a big sigh of relief. Of course, Hiro didn't tell me where she went or anything. Or why.

But now he won't stop talking about her.

It's like she's still sleeping on his couch. He'll just bring up random references to Heaven when the conversation hasn't been calling for it (do our conversations ever?). And today he combed through the papers obsessively – something he doesn't do very much.

I think he's looking for stories about her.

When he brought her up yesterday out of nowhere, I'd just about had it. I said, "Why are you so obsessed with her? What is it, absence makes the heart grow fonder or something?" I know, I know. Real mature. But I couldn't help it. I can't explain.

I also didn't tell him about the fight we had in the park. That I've told her to stay away. But she hasn't.

She doesn't care.

I know what she wants.

Hiro looked at me for a long, long time, not saying anything. "You should be thankful for her," he said finally. "She saved you, remember?"

Then I let out a long scream and went home and threw myself on the bed, crying silently. This is what he always says. "Oh, she saved you, I was so worried that I even sent her in there to fight those guys." Meanwhile, does he have any idea what it was like to be kidnapped by them? To be stuck with them for three days? Alone, scared? While they chattered away in Japanese? They kept me blindfolded the whole time!

But no. It's all about Heaven's needs.

When Hiro tried to call and (I assume) apologize, I let the phone ring and ring and ring and ring. Finally I answered. I tried to explain myself rationally.

Hiro said, "No, no, it's not like that – you're the one I want to be with." I finally relented and went over to his house. We made up, more or less. But I felt uneasy.

Still, I spent the night. Hiro was so loving. I thought, well, maybe this can turn around. Maybe the thing with Heaven was all in my head. And in the morning he goes to work and promises we'll have a romantic dinner together later, and I'm all excited, and I hang around the house for a while, thinking what a silly girl I've been, and the phone rings. And I pick up.

And it's Heaven.

Calling from Joshua Tree. The most romantic park ever.

And you know what she tells me? (I'm getting so emotional, I can feel my heart racing, but too bad.) She tells me that she wants Hiro to come and pick *her up. As if this has been some big plan they've hatched and she's all nonchalant about it, thinking that I know! What have they been saying about me behind my back? Is this some big joke that I'm not in on? Am I the* butt *of the joke?*

I should've yelled at her again. But I didn't. Yelling wasn't getting through to her. So . . . I was nice.

And she apologized!

The bitch. She's not sorry.

Tell him it's urgent, my ass.

I never even knew I had this kind of anger inside me. I've been pacing back and forth ever since. I got so angry that I disconnected the phone from the wall. And now Hiro is late. Has she got ahold of him somehow, is he going out there? And he won't even call and tell me?

I hear his key in the door now. Okay. He hasn't gone. Still, my fists are curled into purple balls. I look frightful. I glance over at the phone in the kitchen. If she calls again, she won't get through.

Karen

9

I sat in the dark for some time, my heart still beating hard. Last time I talked to Karen, she was completely territorial about Hiro. Sort of like a dog.

But maybe . . . maybe she realized how silly that was. Maybe Hiro explained my situation to her logically so she could understand. Perhaps I'd underestimated her. As I was thinking about this, Teddy came bounding back through the door.

"You're still here," he said. I wondered if he'd sat at the end of the hall the whole time, watching my room. But then I noticed he was carrying a cot with him and some blankets. "What do you say we get some really fancy grub tonight? I checked out the options in the lobby, and it looks like this one restaurant downstairs is really dope."

I shrugged. The prospect of food did sound good, but I was worried someone might see us.

"It's totally private," Teddy went on, answering my unspoken question. "No risk, honest." He was holding something else in his hand, too. A bag, from the boutique downstairs. "I bought you something to wear tonight. Instead of the tube top. I thought you might be getting a little cold. I mean, if you want to wear it, that is . . ."

I opened the bag and saw that it was the black Chloé dress I'd had my eye on. It was cool and modern and layered and reminded me of the cool kogyaru girls in Tokyo in all their layered clothes. I turned over the price tag. It was in my size. And *expensive*. I gaped up at him.

"Are you *sure*?" I said. "This is beautiful!"

I couldn't believe Teddy was being so thoughtful. He could have bought me something superscary, like the thong-underwear kind of costumes the girls wear on rap videos, or something that was total leather, or . . .

"You like it?" Teddy asked. "I got myself a button-down shirt, too. I didn't think they'd let me in wearing this getup I've got on now."

God, was this the same Teddy I was hearing? Mr Ghetto Boy Rapper Jay-Z Wanna-be In The Club was now Mr . . . I don't know . . . Brooks Brothers? I glanced down at my dress again. It had been a million years since I'd worn a dress. I'd never even worn one around Hiro. He'd only seen me in casual clothes and workout stuff.

Hiro. A nervous feeling shot through my chest. Would he call me back? How would I answer the phone so Teddy didn't see?

Shit. I should have told him a specific time to call.

Unless . . . unless he just showed up.

I took a luxurious bubble bath while Teddy watched TV, thinking all the while about Hiro. My legs and body felt sore from the botched fight last night. I looked at all the bruises on my shoulders and torso. I wondered what Hiro would have thought of my terrible fighting. And my drinking: Hiro never drank. Said it was a poison, said it made you weak.

Why had Karen acted like such a freak on the phone? Why had she been supernice?

I didn't get it.

Had Hiro told her that I was supposed to forget him? Was she just faking me out?

I slipped out of the tub, still feeling hopeful. The dress hung on the back of the door. I eyed it cautiously. Teddy was trying to buy me into marrying him, but there was something else there, too. Something tender.

I sighed and slid the dress over my head. I gazed at myself in the mirror. I didn't have any styling products or make-up, but somehow it didn't matter. The dress offset my skin tone and hugged my body perfectly. I drew my breath in. It had been so long since I'd worn nice clothes. And it was such a relief to put on something other than the jeans I'd been wearing for three or four days straight.

I came out of the room slowly. Teddy's mouth dropped open. "Heaven," he whispered. He opened his mouth to say something further, but nothing came out. He didn't look bad either in his new button-down shirt. He'd bought himself new trousers, too. "Girl, you clean up nice," he said.

At dinner Teddy continued his gentleman act to such perfection that I began to think it wasn't an act at all. He picked up a roll and buttered it.

"I have to apologize to you for the way I acted on our . . . wedding day. I was a mad coward. I thought those guys were after me or my father. I never thought it was your brother who was the target. I just went on instinct. I'm sorry."

I thought back to the wedding, when Teddy had used me as a shield, leaving me totally exposed to the ninja's attacks.

"My dad and I were messed up in some stuff around that time. I thought that was what was going down," Teddy went on. "I didn't know . . ."

He cleared his throat. "Also, if I knew you then the way I know you now, I would have never, *ever* have done what I did. I would take a bullet for you, Heaven. I would never have thrown you to the wolves. I would protect you from anything." He looked at me very sincerely. A little shiver ran up my spine.

I couldn't believe it. Teddy was more smitten than I'd thought.

But Teddy kept going. "And Heaven, I have to tell you,

since I've come to know you better . . . I . . ." He blushed. I blushed, too. He looked so sweet trying to explain his feelings. Almost sexy. His hair didn't look so brassy, his face didn't look so bulldoggish and thuggish, his body didn't look so huge and beefy. He looked . . . masculine. Rugged.

I wondered if Teddy and I, under other circumstances, might have got together. If we hadn't been forced on each other, if our families hadn't been so screwed up, if we hadn't been running from our own separate demons. I sighed.

"Do you really know nothing about what happened at the wedding?" I asked him. It was a question I'd asked him quite a few times before, and he'd said the same thing every time.

"No way," Teddy said. "I really thought that it might have something to do with my dad and me, but then . . . when the attention was, like, all on you and your bro . . ." He trailed off. "That was a long time ago," he said.

"I didn't like you very much back then," I said. "You were so . . ."

"Yeah," Teddy said, even though I hadn't finished my thought.

"Those engagement parties," I went on. "What was that all about?"

Teddy shrugged. "You weren't exactly the warmest person to be around, either."

"I was sort of icy, wasn't I?" I said softly. My father had tried to make Teddy and me go on walks together to "get to know each other". I'd always refused.

"Well, we just didn't mix, you know? Not at first," Teddy said.

I changed the subject. "So, the attacks weren't on you or your father. They were on me . . . or . . . or my brother. What do you know about my family? Do you have any suspicions about who might have arranged it? Since you're so . . . connected."

Teddy shrugged. "Ohiko found out about your old man. He told him what was on his mind. Well, Konishi wouldn't take that for an answer. I had even heard that Ohiko was into the idea for a while, when he was younger. But then once he started samurai training, all notions of that flew out the window. He changed his mind. He didn't want to do what your father did, no matter how much money and prestige it would bring."

When I heard the words *samurai training*, I froze. *Hiro*. I'd forgotten for a moment.

"I'd met your father before our engagement," Teddy continued, "when I was inducted. My family wasn't on very good terms with your dad, but we had to meet with him sometimes for business reasons. Who was in control of what area of the industry, that sort of thing. We suggested a partnership in loan-sharking. Your father turned it down. It was in Vegas, actually."

"Really?" I said. "Why did he turn it down?"

"I don't know. I mean, he had some dealings in drugs, but loan-sharking . . . he didn't want to get into it. At least not here, stateside."

x

125

Interesting.

"I've heard some stuff about your mom."

"Mieko?" I asked, my heart beating faster. "What have you heard about *her*?"

"Actually, it was in relation to her brother, Masato . . . I don't know if they were tied to yakuza or just aided in yakuza dealings." He paused for a minute and looked at me curiously.

"There's something weird about Masato?" I'd only met Masato once or twice. I hadn't thought of him in years.

"I don't exactly know," Teddy said. "It was just something I heard a while ago, but maybe I'm wrong. Do you know how your parents met, why they got married?"

I didn't. They'd never really seemed married, either. They were never affectionate around Ohiko and me. Of course, perhaps that was out of discretion. I didn't know. As far as I knew, they slept in the same bedroom together. Ohiko and I used to joke around about them – how they seemed like a cardboard couple. Totally fake. But Ohiko *was* their birth son, so they must have . . . just once . . .

"I don't, either," Teddy said. "I don't even know about my own parents."

I thought about Teddy's mother. She hadn't been around much during the wedding preparations. She lived in the Yukemura house in Nice. I couldn't even remember if she'd been there on the wedding day. She had to have been, right?

Our dinners came, and we took the time to put our napkins on our laps and ogle the food and dig in. I had salmon – it was delicious. I couldn't remember the last time I'd had an elaborate sit-down meal like this.

"But really, seeing that shit go down at the wedding was the shock of my life," Teddy said after a little while. "I was so upset that I just bounced outta there . . . didn't help you or nothing."

"No one helped me," I said flatly. "Everyone just stood there. But whatever." I shrugged. "What can we do about it now?"

"Still," Teddy said, looking at me with remorse. "I'm sorry. You don't know how sorry I am."

I didn't say anything, but I was touched.

"And . . . there's something else," Teddy went on. "Back when we first met up in L.A., I was trying in many ways to capture you so that we could marry. I had my finger on the trigger. I arranged for the ambush In front of your friend Hiro's house. I was trying to think of anything. I even tried to reason with you – ya know? But you were stubborn. But I've changed. Word up. You should know that by the fact that I helped you. I let you out of getting married. I let you free. But this time I mean it. I'm furilla. I want to be serious."

I took a deep breath, then took a sip of water. "Well, I have to say, when I came over here for the wedding, I thought marrying you was a fate worse than death. And I didn't even know half of what was going on in my family or yours. But now . . . well . . . now if I could rewind it, in many ways it would have been better if we would have just got married then, before all of this happened to us."

Teddy nodded.

We fell into silence and ate the rest of our dinner. Teddy had admitted his feelings to me. Who had ever admitted feelings to me before? When had I had a true, honest conversation with someone? Not my father. Not Hiro – especially nothing ever romantic. Ohiko, yes. Katie, yes. But it felt like it had been so long. Even last night with Katie felt hurried and stressful. I smiled at him from across the table. It felt like we were allies.

We walked, exhausted, back to the room. "You wanna watch TV?" Teddy asked.

"Sure," I said.

Teddy unfolded the cot for himself. He actually was going to sleep on it. I was amazed. Who was this new Teddy? He had totally mellowed out. He flipped on MTV and, to my surprise, started to watch an episode of *Sorority Life*. I'd watched this a couple of times with Cheryl.

"You *like* this show?" I said, laughing.

Teddy shrugged. "It's much more interesting than *Fraternity Life*, that's for sure."

I bit my lip. Teddy's affinity for cheesy TV shows was kind of charming. Hiro didn't watch television.

"That one girl is like mega-pledge," Teddy said, pointing

at one of the girls who was pouring her heart out on the screen.

Hiro would probably say this kind of television was drivel. We both sat transfixed by the idiotic events that were unfolding on-screen.

Suddenly a thought drove into my head.

Hiro. Had he called?

My pulse started to race. I waited until Teddy had fallen asleep – he *snored*! – and then checked my cell phone. Nothing. No messages. No missed calls. As Teddy slept, I snuck into the hall and dialled Hiro's number again on my cell phone. It was busy. Hopefully Karen had given him the message. I hung up the phone and went back into the room to sleep.

The next day Teddy and I lazed around the pool and walked through the park again. We watched a whole marathon of *Sorority Life*. I kept sneaking into the hallway (claiming to get ice, candy bars, soda, whatever) to call and check the messages. Nothing. No red lights, no blinking, no missed calls. No notes at the front desk. I scanned the road for Hiro. Nothing. *Where was he?*

I dialled his number again and again. I must have dialled it twenty times. It was always busy. "What the hell?" I said out loud to the empty room. Hiro could have taken the phone off the hook to prevent me from calling again. God, maybe he really didn't want me to come back. My spirits dropped.

Later that night I snuck into the hall to try the line again. I couldn't think of Karen's number, and information didn't have it listed. She'd probably changed her number after her kidnapping. I began to realize that Hiro wasn't coming. He was serious. I was to forget him. I really had to do this on my own.

I lay in bed again that next night. Teddy drifted quickly into sleep, but I stayed awake, terrified. I crept into the hall with my phone and dialled the number one more time.

It rang.

My heart started to pound. This was the first time the call had gone through. I checked my watch. It wasn't too late, only about eleven-thirty. It rang once more, and then I heard a voice.

"Hello?"

It was Karen.

I opened my mouth to speak, but I was frozen with fear. She sounded totally pissed off. I heard Hiro's voice in the background. Before I knew what I was doing, I hung up.

They hadn't gone anywhere. They'd just taken the phone off the hook, hoping I wouldn't call. Karen's kindness must have been an act.

How dare Hiro just drop me like this? Wasn't this totally against the bushido code? Wasn't he supposed to be looking out for me? How could he be so . . . heartless? Had some sort of terrible spirit occupied his body, telling him that he must never, ever speak to me again? What was the point of even taking me in the first place if this was going to be the end result?

I tossed and turned in bed in a rage, feeling angrier and angrier with Hiro. Finally, worn out, I decided I couldn't think about it anymore. I had to formulate a new plan for myself.

I had to move to plan B.

10

I was standing on the edge of a canyon in Joshua Tree Park. There was no one around. The sun was coming up, making the rocks red and gold. It was gorgeous. I was wearing the Chloé dress that Teddy had bought me. My hair was up. I wore new shoes. I felt like a princess.

Hiro appeared. He wore a swanky suit and his hair looked like it had been cut and styled. It even looked like he had highlights. He smiled broadly at me.

"You came!" I breathed in. I was ecstatic.

"I'm here," he said. "It took me two days, but I'm here."

I gave him a hug. "It's been terrible without you," he told me. "My world was just crumbling. I had no idea . . ."

"It's all right," I said.

A shadow fell over us. There was Teddy, dressed in a long robe. His hair was arranged in disturbing, devil-like spikes on his head. He was holding, of all things, a torch. In the other hand, he was holding the Whisper of Death.

"Teddy!" I said. He was staring at me. He looked angry.

"Hello, Hiro," Teddy said. "I see you've come for Heaven."

Hiro didn't say anything. I saw him move into a battle stance. Crouched down, his arms in front of him, his back tense.

"Teddy, what's all this about?" I said.

Teddy looked at me. He had some weird sort of turquoise paint on his face. It swirled out from his nose and curled around his ears. It looked completely bizarre. "Well, Heaven, you said that you would give Hiro forty-eight hours. Two days. And his two days are up. Now I have to eliminate him."

"What?" I said. "What are you talking about?"

Hiro turned to me. "You made a promise in your head?" he said. "You only gave me two days? Don't you realize it takes two days to drive here?"

But it didn't take two days to drive from L.A. to Joshua Tree. Even I knew that. I stood there, tongue-tied. Another fig-ure stepped from behind Teddy. A smaller, stealthier figure.

Ninja.

To be more precise, the ninja from the wedding. I recog-nized the crest on his obi.

I gasped.

The ninja's eyes glowed an eerie shade of red. He stared

133

right at me. *"So, we meet again,"* he said to me. *"Hello, Heaven Kogo."*

I opened my mouth, but no sound came out.

The ninja walked closer to Hiro and me. I looked at Hiro. Do something! I wanted to tell him. He looked terrified. He stood there, completely disarmed. I trembled.

"You gave Hiro forty-eight hours," the ninja said. *"That's not very much time, is it?"*

"Well . . . ," I started.

The ninja held up his hand to silence me. "You gave him forty-eight hours, and now his forty-eight hours are up. Now he must die."

"No!" I said. Teddy handed the Whisper of Death to the ninja. They're in cahoots? I thought angrily, looking fiercely back and forth from Teddy to the ninja. Hiro stood there, as if he were in suspended animation. "Move, Hiro!" I yelled. But Hiro was frozen.

My eyes flew open. Sweat had soaked the sheets. How long had I been sleeping? What time was it?

I raised my head. Teddy was still asleep. The clock said six-thirty. I had been tossing and turning all night, trying to figure out what to do. Hiro really wasn't coming for me. I had to make a plan for myself. I thought I'd figured out something good, although after that dream . . .

But no. Teddy had told me truthfully that he was on my side. I really *did* believe him.

I had a plan B. It involved Teddy.

I heard the rustling of sheets. Teddy sat up straight and looked at me. "Hey," he said.

"Hey," I answered, covering myself with the blanket. I went to the bathroom quickly and stared at myself in the mirror. *Okay. You have to do this. It's plan B.*

I stared at my features. My skin was looking tired and worn out. My eyes were puffy from lack of sleep. My hair was standing every which way. At least my black eye had faded. I tried to smooth my hair down a little and straighten out my T-shirt. I pulled on my jeans and went back into the room.

Teddy had put on his jeans, too. "You're up early," he said. "I guess we can see the morning sun this way."

"Teddy," I said in a loud voice, perhaps to sound convincing, perhaps to rouse myself from the weird dreams I'd been having.

"I've decided," I continued. "I've thought about it long and hard. We should get married and go back to L.A."

Teddy stared at me. My heart pounded.

His jaw dropped open and he broke into a gigantic smile. "Are you serious?" he said.

"Yeah . . . of course." I tried a smile.

He blinked a couple of times. "Whoa, Heaven. I'm . . . I'm amazed." He stood up and took my hands. *"Really?"*

"Yes," I said, now smiling wider.

Teddy gave me a gigantic hug. "This is great," he said. I could tell he was really overwhelmed. "We've . . . we've got to get out of here, then. Let's go back to L.A. now, today. Let's pack up and leave."

"Okay," I said. My heart raced. The sooner we went, the better.

It didn't take us long to pack up. All I really had was my dress, my purse, my extra underwear, and my sleeping T-shirt. Days had passed and I'd survived on a couple of things from a bag and had been to Vegas and back. Pretty amazing. I wondered, fleetingly, what Katie was doing right now. Had she just got back from a party? Was she sleeping? Was she thinking about me? Was she shell-shocked? Had she called the police?

We walked into the lobby. Teddy quickly went to the front desk and paid for the room and the dinner and the clothes that he'd bought at the gift shop with his credit card – I guess it was all itemized into one bill. "Let me help with that," I said.

"No way," he answered. He looked at me and smiled. "You're gonna be my wife. You won't have to pay for anything."

In the car Teddy leaned over and gave me a kiss. Up close, he didn't smell so bad – sort of like cinnamon and clove cigarettes. He started up the engine and we drove off. I fidgeted with everything in the car – the windows, the locks, the glove compartment. "Nervous?" Teddy said.

"Me? No. Not a bit." I smiled back. "I really think this is a good decision after all."

"Yeah," Teddy said. "So, you want to like have a big ceremony or anything or just make it really small?"

I looked at him like he was crazy. "Would it be *smart* for us to have a big ceremony? Considering our . . . our track record?" I felt a twinge about that dream I'd had last night. The ninja.

Teddy paused for a traffic signal. "Yeah, you're probably right." He smiled. "Too bad we can't go back to Vegas. We could go to a twenty-four-hour chapel. You know, Elvis's house of love or something like that."

I laughed. "Yeah," I said. "Well, a small ceremony, then. But no Vegas."

Teddy hummed along to the radio while I sat and played with the lock-unlock button. My heart was still racing.

We drove down a long, unbroken highway. All around us was desert and heat. Pretty depressing, but Teddy was on cloud nine, singing along to a Limp Bizkit song. "Hey, you hear that 'Heaven's Gone' song yet?" Teddy asked me. "Can you believe that shit? As soon as we're married, I'm going to get them to pull that from the air. I don't want anyone else singing about you."

"I haven't heard it," I lied.

"Well, you can't really understand it anyway; it's all in Japanese and mumbled, too. It's not as if anyone here is going to understand what they're saying – hey, what's that in front of us?"

I looked out on the horizon. There was a helicopter

heading straight for the highway. "That's weird," I said. "What do you think it's doing?"

"It's flying awfully low," Teddy said. He adjusted the dial on the radio.

I tensed up. Something about the helicopter reminded me of my dream.

The helicopter dipped farther and farther, finally looking like it was going to land right on the highway. "Dude," Teddy said. "Maybe it's in trouble." He slowed the car down as the helicopter settled on the ground, its propeller kicking up clouds of dust. The other cars in front of us skidded either around it or off the road. A couple of cars ended up on the shoulder.

"What do you think . . . ," Teddy started. The helicopter's propeller still whirled, but it was firmly settled on the ground now. And then something incredible happened.

From the helicopter emerged one ninja after another. Cloaked in head-to-toe black.

I counted fast. Ten of them.

"Ouch," Teddy whispered.

They were coming right for us.

I quickly looked at Teddy. He looked back at me and nodded. We had to act fast. These guys wanted both of us.

The first group of three approached me with some low-flying mae geri kicks. I dodged them. Luckily I was feeling a little more together this time, as opposed to my drunken awkward fight in front of Katie's house.

I gave the first guy a solid kick to the stomach. Even though I hadn't been training for a little while, I still felt pretty strong. I think it surprised them – they were probably expecting that with my smaller frame, I'd be an easy victory. The guy staggered backwards, surprised.

But then the next guy jumped on me from behind. I felt his weight on my back and the air was completely knocked out of me. Suddenly I was on the ground. The ninja, breathing heavily, managed to roll me over despite my kicking so that he was on top of me. That was when I made my move. Before he could settle in (and before he could start hitting me), I twisted his body and flipped him over so that I had full access to his throat. Then I started to put him in a choke hold.

The guy flailed and suddenly lost consciousness. Another ninja was dragging me by the hair. I screamed and let go of the other guy, rolling his heavy body off me. I leapt to my feet. The ninja was ready, knocking me down with a hane goshi move – a throw off his hip. I rolled back up quickly, wincing in pain, and countered with a blow to his shoulder. He raced towards me, but I backed up. Suddenly there was a crack on my spine. Someone was behind me.

I whirled around and tiger-punched the next ninja in his throat. He gasped for air. I manoeuvered over to the spinning blades of the helicopter – they hadn't turned the ignition off. I could use the shadows to my advantage by using the shinobi-iri methods of invisibility. I had done this before to slide into the shadows and trick my enemy. Hopefully it would work again.

I glanced over at Teddy. He had pulled out his gun and was waving it around at the ninjas. They backed away. Even *I* backed away. But then Teddy tried to fire it, and nothing happened. Just an empty clicking noise.

"Shit," Teddy muttered. The gun didn't have any bullets.

He threw the weapon down and switched tactics, pulling out his knives from under his shirt. Before the ninjas even knew what was going on, he slashed two of them.

Where had he been keeping those knives?

I had to concentrate. Only one ninja was down and the others were hungry. One advanced towards me with a long, thin knife in his hand. I slid into the shadows and managed to elude him. I knocked the knife out of his hand. It skidded over in Teddy's direction.

"Teddy!" I yelled, then gestured towards the knife. He grabbed it.

The ninjas, being much more schooled in martial arts than I was, also knew about shinobi-iri. They could slide in and out of the shadows, too. They weren't like the Yukemura clan, brutish and reliant on their weapons. These guys were experts. I slid into one shadow and bumped haphazardly into one of my assailants. Luckily Teddy was right behind us, pulling out his knife, slashing him across the shoulder. Then he punched him in the face. The ninja dropped like a stone.

I was kicked from the back again and went flailing to the ground. All at once pain came from all angles, affecting every part of me. My neck. My back. My legs. I felt my organs being crushed. Who was this? I looked up. Two ninjas. Where was Teddy?

Suddenly Teddy's shadow fell over them, and he grabbed both by their shoulders and whipped them backward (I'd honestly had no idea that Teddy was so strong). One ninja, however, wasn't impressed. He lunged at Teddy and flipped him. Teddy crashed to the ground. I heard him heaving, the wind knocked out of him. When his breath came back, he wailed in pain.

I tried to sit up, spitting out blood. I managed to stand and walk over to Teddy. "Get up," I said, offering him a hand. "Come on." Teddy staggered to his feet. There was only one ninja left standing.

The ninja started to shake as he realized that we outnumbered him. The other men lay In pools of blood or were simply unconscious. Teddy shoved his knives back into his pockets but kept the ninja's out in front of him. He waved it to the ninja.

"You want some more?" he growled. The ninja glared at us. "Who are you?" I shouted. "Who sent you?" The ninja brushed by us before we could react and scampered into the helicopter.

"Hey!" Teddy said, rushing towards the vehicle. "Hey!"

The propellers began to spin faster. The ninja manned

the controls and the whole thing began to lift off the ground. Teddy stood below it, trying to jump up and hang on to the copter's bottom.

"Don't!" I yelled at him.

The helicopter climbed higher into the sky. The ninja was leaving his nine other men for dead. Teddy walked back to me, staring at them. None were moving, although I doubted we'd killed any of them. "Should we keep one as our prisoner? Make him answer our questions?" he asked.

"I think we should get the hell out of here," I said. My heart was racing. Teddy and I had fended off nine ninjas, but I couldn't help but realize that if it hadn't been for Teddy's dirty street-fighting skills, we'd still be trying to battle them. Or worse – losing. They were better fighters than I was. I began to cough madly, spitting up more blood.

"They were really kicking you," Teddy said. "Are you all right?"

"I think so," I said. They'd freshened all the bruises from the fight in front of Katie's house – I'd been beaten much worse then. Honestly, I felt like crying, my body hurt so badly. But I didn't want to for some reason. Perhaps it was the bushi code inside me telling me not to – don't show any emotion. Be strong.

Our eyes stung with dust. We watched the helicopter soar out of view. Teddy clenched his fists, breathing in and out. His T-shirt was stained red with blood – some of his own, some of the ninjas'. We didn't say anything for a long time. Luckily none of the ninjas on the ground stirred. Maybe we *had* killed some of them.

Teddy reached down and picked up the gun, examining it. "I guess I fired off more bullets than I thought that night in front of your friend's house," he said. I shuddered. I didn't like being so close to a gun, loaded or unloaded. Teddy shoved it in his pocket. "I don't think L.A.'s such a good idea anymore."

I thought about my plan B. What would I do now?

Then, in the distance, a figure appeared. It looked like it was riding a motorcycle. When it got closer, I could hear the low, grumbling hum of a bike. The figure looked ominous.

My body tensed, ready for action.

"What's coming?" I said to Teddy. Teddy didn't answer.

The motorcycle growled closer. I squinted. The figure looked familiar. A ninja I'd fought before? A Yukemura thug? I looked at Teddy but then thought, *Nah, I don't think he's tricking me.*

The rider looked familiar, though. He got closer and closer, and I couldn't figure out who it was. *Who do I know who has a motorcycle? No one.*

"I know that guy," Teddy said.

The rider was very close now.

"Dude, isn't that . . . ?" Teddy said. He looked at me, confused.

It was. My heart leaped.

Hiro.

She says she'll marry me.

I couldn't believe she didn't bail out on me. I totally thought that when I was gettin' a little shut-eye, Heaven would break my heart and sneak away, but she didn't. Every day I'd wake up and there she'd be, lying on that bed like a princess, and today, this morning of all mornings, she says she'll marry me.

Boo-ya!

I mean, before it was, like, awesome, bling bling rollin' my way, that fat wad that was promised me for baggin' Heaven Kogo. But now . . .

Getting married is when life starts to mean something. I didn't realize this when it was first, you know, like, an order. When all that mad ceremonious stuff was happenin', when there was party after party, when all that was goin' down, I barely noticed Heaven, I must admit. Yeah, yeah, whatever, her dad's a gangster and she's a little bitch princess. I admit it. I'd never tell her this in so many words, but that's what I thought.

But now, well . . . everything's changed.

I wanted to have a ring to give her. I want to give her everything. When I bought her that dress, damn. She looked fine. *She was the most beautiful thing I'd ever seen, and this was after she got the shit kicked out of her the day before, this was after riding in the car for hours, this was after all the stress she'd gone through, everything. And she still looked like a million bucks.*

This is just . . . this is just amazing, is what it is. I feel better than I did after anything I've ever pumped into my body, any little snort or joint or whatever.

This is the real vibe.

As we drive, she's superquiet. Maybe thinking about wife stuff or like what kind of dress she's gonna get.

Shit – maybe she's thinking about sex!

Has she had sex?

But then this helicopter lands in the middle of the road, and we're sitting here, and it's like Mission Impossible, and I realize I have to keep my promise to her – I have to protect her from anything. I have to . . . I have to fight these dudes! But what's really messed up is, I think deep down Heaven's way tougher than me. She'd probably be better at protecting me than I am at protecting her. She probably wasn't sitting there in the car thinking about wifely stuff and all that shit. She was probably thinking about something else. Something more dangerous. She probably would never think about wifely shit.

And that's why I love her. Although I'd never tell her that.

Teddy

11

The motorcycle slowed, kicking up dust. I couldn't believe my eyes. It really was Hiro. He dismounted and stared at us. He was wearing a black jacket, boots. The motorcycle was a little ragged looking but still sexy.

He looked better than ever. I don't know how, exactly – I'd only seen him, what, four days ago, but somehow he looked . . . different. Older. Wiser. I didn't know.

Hiro looked around, his mouth hanging open. "I – I was coming to Joshua Tree," he said to me. "I thought you were . . ." Then he stopped. "What happened?"

My heart lifted. He *was* coming to get me!

Hiro gaped first at the ninjas strewn around the road (the cars on the highway were swerving around them, bleating out confused beeps. Far away I could hear a siren, which meant we should split soon, otherwise we'd be in even bigger trouble), then at Teddy, looming above me. "Okay," he said slowly. He looked back at me. "I only got your message this morning. I'm sorry."

"What, were you out of town?" I asked, as impassively as I could. I thought about Karen fielding that phone call. What had happened?

"No – no." Hiro looked a little at a loss for words. "I'll explain. But not right now. What happened? What's going on? Where are you two headed? Are you in danger, Heaven? Why are you with Teddy?"

Neither of us said anything. Teddy glared at Hiro, but he was still out of breath from the fighting. Teddy's size and lack of exercise made him a brute strength sort of fighter. But he lost stamina quickly. He still hadn't recovered, while I was feeling okay. I remembered Teddy's words in Katie's apartment: "Let's not get him involved." I was sure he wasn't particularly thrilled that Hiro had shown up.

Finally I sputtered: "So . . . if you weren't anywhere . . . what happened? Why did you only get the message this morning?" My hands were on my hips.

"What message?" Teddy finally barked. He straightened up.

"Karen had been keeping the message from me," Hiro said sheepishly. "You called a couple of days ago, right?"

"That's right," I said. Of *course* Karen hadn't been serious when she'd put on that "sweetie pie" voice. She'd been totally going to screw me over!

"She kept the message from me but let it slip this morning during a big fight we were having." He looked down.

Karen, Hiro, fight? "What were you fighting about?" I asked quietly.

The moment suddenly became very charged. Hiro looked up into my eyes. His expression was one of clarity, understanding. Maybe even a little remorse.

"You," he said.

My whole body melted, then, in its puddle state, shivered. *What* did he just say? Was I hallucinating? Had the ninjas killed me in the battle? Was I *dead*?

"Whoa, whoa," Teddy said, finally gathering his composure, waving his arms back and forth as if to stop the conversation. "What's going on here?"

But Hiro and I stared at each other as if we'd slipped into another dimension. Time and sound and speed slowed down. We were in our own little block of ice. Nothing could break our gaze. I stared at him, dumbstruck. Had he said . . . ? He wore a look of . . . I'm not sure what it was. He looked . . . *amorous*. Like they do in the movies.

Surely this was some sort of test.

"She . . . she said I was obsessed with you," Hiro said. His voice even sounded trancelike. "She had disconnected the phone. And the one message you left, she never gave it to me. She was jealous. And . . . well . . . she had good reason to be, I guess."

148

"Excuse me?" Teddy said. "Hello? What's going on here? What do you want, bro?"

They were breaking up. They had broken up. Oh my God. I'd never imagined this. Never in a million years. I'd thought they'd get married and have children and . . . and . . .

This was so unbelievably surreal. Like those pictures of melting clocks. I cleared my throat, continued to stare at Hiro. I felt a hand on my back and jumped. It was Teddy.

"Heaven," he said in a powerful voice. "We have to get out of here. Those sirens? Those are for us."

I nodded, still transfixed. Hiro was still staring at me.

"They might even have backup," Teddy went on, his voice quavering. He must have sensed something of what was happening between Hiro and me but seemed completely confused as to how to handle it. He tugged on my arm. "We've got to go. They probably tracked me from Joshua Tree to here." He hit himself on the head. "We're in danger if we stay here for another moment."

I didn't move.

Teddy looked over at Hiro, who hadn't moved, either. He still held on to his bike.

"Look, man, hanging around with us will do you no good," Teddy said, puffing up his chest. "I don't know what you're tryin' to pull here, like what kind of message you got or whatever . . . Who knows, maybe it was from whoever just choppered down and karate-kicked us . . . But you've got to go. Back to L.A. or wherever you came from. Heaven and I, we gotta split. We can't go back to L.A. now. We were planning to, but . . ." Teddy shrugged.

Hiro remained placid and still. "I'm not leaving," he said. "I'm going with you."

A million little fireworks went off in my body at once.

Teddy shrugged angrily. He looked at me pleadingly. "What's his *deal*?" he sputtered, his voice squeaking a little. "Can you, like, call him off? Send him packing?"

I shook my head ever so slightly. "I don't think so," I said.

"I'm coming," Hiro said, his voice growing a little stronger, not so trancelike. "But we should get out of here. L.A. is dangerous. I'm assuming Vegas is dangerous. Anywhere in California is bad news. Really, we should leave the country. That would be best."

"What's all this 'we' stuff?" Teddy said.

"We could get passports," I said feebly.

"Yeah. Easier said than done," Teddy said. "Two passports maybe, but not three."

"Nowhere is safe in this country." Hiro looked at Teddy. "You should know this. You're in danger and on the run as much as Heaven. More so, really. So can you get us access to passports so that we can go somewhere in Europe?"

"Europe?" I said.

Teddy glowered, kicked at some dust. He paced around in a large circle, walking over to his car, kicking the tire. He let out a long, frustrated grunt. Hiro and I watched him silently. Then his ears pricked up at the approaching sirens. "Fine," he said, walking back to us. "I guess I can do that. We'll have to go to Mexico to get them. I know someone . . . but I don't think he can swing three."

"Hiro has to come," I heard myself saying.

Teddy gaped at me. "He does, does he? Why? I don't get this!"

"Because . . . ," I tried to explain.

"I'm her sensei," Hiro said.

Of course. All this *was* a samurai test. I knew it. He was my sensei. Of course.

"Ooh, and what does that mean?" Teddy asked in a teasing voice. "Heaven with a sensei. Who is she, Buffy? And am I Angel?"

"Look, we can either stand here and argue like children or we can save ourselves," Hiro said calmly. "Now, can you get three passports?"

Teddy hesitated, looking back and forth from Hiro to me. My heart was nearly jumping out of my chest. Why did Hiro want to come along so badly? Was he leaving Karen for good? If he left the country and got on our dangerous bandwagon, he'd be leaving his life in L.A . . . for me.

Finally, after Hiro had stared Teddy down for a good five minutes, Teddy admitted, "Fine. I think I probably could."

"I thought you could," Hiro said.

"But why do you . . . ," I started, looking at Hiro. Hiro put his hand on his lips, a gesture for me to be quiet.

"We have to move," Hiro said. "Is that your car?" He gestured to Teddy's vehicle, turned at an odd angle because of the helicopter landing in the middle of the road. Teddy nodded. Hiro waved his hands. "Let's go, then."

"What about your bike?" I said.

Hiro looked at it, then wheeled it over to a deep ditch and pushed it in.

Teddy turned to me when Hiro was out of earshot. "Yo, Heaven, what the hell?" he said angrily. "Why doesn't he go back to L.A.?"

"Teddy, Hiro is as connected to me as you are. Now, they might be after you for whatever you've done wrong, but they're after me, too. Together we're a jackpot. I mean, realistically, since Hiro is the person I've been closest to in L.A., if I go missing, they might attack him. It's probably safer for him to come with us."

There. A logical answer for why Hiro had trekked out here and left his life behind. The more I thought about it, the more it made total sense. Hiro wasn't looking at me like a sick puppy because he had some kind of feelings for me. He needed to save himself. If that meant sacrificing Karen, then that was what he had to do.

But he'd said . . .

It must have been a ploy of some sort.

Teddy grumbled. "What do I care if it's safer for him? I might not even be able to get hold of passports for us.

What'll I do then? We'll be stuck in Mexico. And it's *mad* dangerous there."

"Teddy, of course you can get passports," I said. "You even said the other night at dinner that getting fake IDs and passports was one of the easiest things to do if you had the right connections."

"Yeah, but . . ." Teddy kicked at the dust again, scowling. "What was this *message* you left for him? Did I hear that correctly? I didn't see any calls to L.A. on our bill."

"It was . . . it was . . . I didn't exactly know what was going to happen, Teddy," I admitted. "I mean, when we got to Joshua Tree, I didn't quite trust you, and . . . I didn't think Hiro was really going to show up." I looked at him. Teddy looked hurt.

I felt a little awkward here. We'd become a team. And then Hiro, who was the love of my life – another thing Teddy didn't know – showed up, saying I'd left him a message, and here he was. But I'd betrayed Teddy. I'd gone behind his back: I'd basically called out for help to get me out of there. I'd mistrusted him. I wasn't sure how angry this would make him. But I had a feeling that he would know better than to desert us, or worse, to try and hurt us. We were better fighters than Teddy was. And I knew for a fact that his gun didn't have any bullets in it.

Or did it?

Hiro walked back to the car. "Come on," he said. "You want to drive?" he asked Teddy.

153

"It's my car, isn't it?" Teddy said gruffly.

"Drive us to a side road and then pull over so you can call around about the passports," Hiro instructed.

Teddy glared at him. "I can talk and drive at the same time," he said. "I *did* live in L.A. It's really *not* that hard."

We piled in the car. I got into the back first, thinking Hiro would want the front with Teddy. But then, to my surprise, Hiro climbed into the backseat beside me.

"Yo, what the hell?" Teddy said angrily, turning his head around to see us in the backseat. "I'm not your chauffeur!"

"Drive!" Hiro said. "I can see the police cars back there."

"Unbelievable . . ." Teddy sped off, cursing under his breath.

I sat very straight in the seat, twisting around to see the fallen ninjas disappearing in the distance.

Teddy whipped out his cell phone and started calling around about passports. "Are you sure you want to use that?" I asked. "Isn't your cell traceable?"

Teddy muttered something I couldn't understand.

I pulled out my phone with the untraceable number. "Use this," I said.

Teddy looked back at me. "How long have you had this phone?" he asked. He looked at it.

"It's the same phone that you called me on when I was in L.A.," I answered. I had a feeling Teddy was putting two and two together: this was how I'd called Hiro from the hotel without the call coming up on the Joshua Tree checkout bill.

Teddy punched in some numbers and began to talk. "Pablo . . . yo! . . . Yeah. Me and my girl want to go to Europe to chill out and shit . . . maybe hit some spas . . . maybe go to Amsterdam . . . some clubs . . . drinkin' . . . yeah." Hiro gave me a strange look. I raised my eyebrows as if to say, *I don't know what's going on.* I hoped Teddy wouldn't mention that I'd told him I'd marry him. Teddy continued. "Yeah, listen, we need to split the crib for a while. No, no, you'll get yo' dinero, no problem, man, it's not that . . . So how about hooking us up with some passports . . . ? Yeah, yeah, we'll come south of the border to get them . . . Why do we need them . . .? Well . . . little vacation, little R and R, ya know? Break from the ghetto."

As if Teddy had an idea what a ghetto was. He'd grown up like a prince. Hiro sat next to me, sort of tense. I peeked over at him. He was sneaking a look at me. I smiled slightly.

"Hey," I said. I giggled. Hiro nodded back, all serious. I quickly looked out the window.

Teddy sped along, driving with one hand. "Listen, yo. I'll pay you your fifty thousand plus an additional amount for these, we're talking cash . . . C'mon, man . . ." He looked frustrated. It didn't sound like Pablo was into the whole thing. I gripped the side of the backseat with my fingers. My heart was racing and being pulled in a million directions. Hiro was here. He'd broken up with Karen.

"I got an idea," Teddy said into the phone, snapping his fingers. "Fake kidnapping. How does that strike you?"

"Fake kidnapping?" Hiro whispered.

"My family will pay anything," Teddy continued. "Whatever you ask. Once we get to TJ, that's when it'll go down. And then you guys will be livin' large in Bora Bora or wherever the hell you want to go. My father spares no expense. It's totally foolproof. A bomb idea, right . . . ? Yeah. Yeah? You will?"

"That doesn't sound like a good idea," Hiro said.

"Solid, brotha," Teddy said before I could answer. "See you in TJ, then. Nice. Niiiiiice. Set it up now. Right. I don't care. Fine. Okay, later." He hung up and turned to face us, a sour look falling over his face when he saw us sitting together in the backseat. "Okay, we're in," he said. "Three Swiss passports. We're going to Tijuana to get them. Does that fly with you, kemo sabe?" He looked at Hiro. Hiro nodded. "I know someone else who can help us get across the border quick. I don't think we'll want to be in TJ for long."

"Switzerland," I said. I'd never been there.

"Yeah. It's the bomb. I was in boarding school there for about six months." He grinned. "And we could check out Amsterdam, too." I was just waiting for him to bring up the marriage. But for the moment he'd forgotten. Perhaps because of the attack and all the excitement about the border problems. I hoped he'd continue to forget. It was a conversation I didn't feel like having. How was I going to tell Hiro that I'd agreed to marry Teddy?

"Okay. So who's getting up front with me now?" Teddy said, patting the passenger's seat. "It'll be a long drive to the border. I need someone to work the radio."

Neither of us moved. We sat in the backseat, a strange, electric current running between us. I looked at Hiro again. He was looking at me. He opened his mouth but didn't say anything. I had so many questions about everything, but I didn't know where to start.

"Hello?" Teddy said in a louder voice. "I said, who's coming up here with me?"

"I think we're fine for now," I said softly. Hiro blinked. Then, ever so slightly, he smiled.

Karen was hiding phone calls from me. I found out about it last night when I came home from work. She was sitting on the couch, reading. We'd had a calm couple of days. We were both trying to be as nice as possible to each other – to work these things out. Then the phone rang.

I recall saying, "Funny, the phone seems like it hasn't rung in days." Karen leapt up to get it. She picked it up and barked into the receiver. Then she glared at me and put the phone back on the cradle.

"Who was it?" I asked.

"No one," she said. "Just a hang-up."

But she gave away something in the way that she said it. She wanted me to ask, to pry. Karen is not a terrible person. Whatever she was doing, she was doing in order to save the relationship.

So I asked. "But you do know who it was," I said. I looked at the caller ID box. It was a 760 number. "Who do we know in the 760 area code?"

"No one," she said. Then, out of nowhere, she broke down. She didn't cry, exactly, she just sort of let all the air escape out of her body. "Please tell me," she said. "Please admit that you are planning on doing something with Heaven at Joshua Tree behind my back. Because I can't stand this sneaking around anymore. I just can't stand any of this anymore."

"Joshua Tree?" I asked. "What are you talking about?" I looked at the area code. Joshua Tree, I remembered, is in the 760 area code. I knew because it is near Palm Springs and I once had to go out there on a retreat with the members of the dojo. Suddenly I felt very faint. "Was that Heaven calling?" I said.

"So you *were* planning something!" she said flatly.

"What?" I said. "I'm not planning anything. I haven't talked to Heaven in a long time. But you have, it seems . . ."

Karen didn't say anything. She looked down at her feet. "I really felt something for you," she said eventually. "She called the other day. She said she was at Joshua Tree. She needed you to come get her. I thought . . . I thought . . . I don't know." Tears sprang up in the corners of her eyes.

"Wait. What?" I sputtered. Heaven in Joshua Tree Park? Why wasn't she in Vegas? What was going on?

"Do you love her?" Karen sniffed.

"How could you have kept that phone call from me? Have you been intercepting others? Why hasn't the phone been ringing?" I felt very strange all of a sudden. Heaven had called. What kind of danger was she in?

"You don't even care," Karen said, "that you've hurt me. This obviously isn't working." She turned and walked out the door.

"Wait!" I yelled. "You don't understand! I don't even know . . ." Karen kept walking. She didn't look back. My head spun. I tried to regain some control. Heaven was at Joshua Tree. Crying out for help. How could Karen have *thought I was planning some secret tryst with her? How could Karen have lied to me?*

The next morning I got ready to leave. I borrowed a motorcycle from a neighbour and packed up a couple of things. I called Karen. I told her I was going away to get Heaven, and then I didn't know where I'd be. I said it was something I had to do. I tried to explain my feelings. She cried a little but said she understood. She said she sensed it coming and apologized for keeping Heaven's message from me. It wasn't a particularly good conversation, but I felt a little better after it was done.

I know I must have a longer, deeper conversation explaining things to Karen. I didn't mean to hurt her. I need to make her understand. I will have to contact her later, perhaps in a letter or something. I tried to think through what I would say to Karen as I took the trip to Joshua Tree. But as I rode off on the motorcycle, I couldn't keep my mind on her. I was thinking about something else. Something strong. Something about Heaven. I hoped I would reach Joshua Tree before it was too late.

Hiro

1 2

We stopped for gas about an hour later. I got out and stretched my legs.

"So are you going to sit up front with me now?" Teddy asked, putting his arms above his head.

"Um . . . ," I said.

"She should sit in the back," Hiro said.

During the first hour Hiro and I had been looking at each other curiously, as if we were two species of animals that had never met. Peals of adrenaline had coursed through me and I felt almost edgy.

"Yeah? Why is that?" Teddy was counting out his bills to pay with cash. He couldn't risk using his credit card again. He'd been very silent during the drive. I could tell he was waiting for an explanation. Perhaps that was why I felt a little edgy: the tension in the car could have been cut with a chain saw.

Hiro paused, waiting to answer. *Say because you love me. Say because you love me.* I tried to send this to Hiro's brain via ESP.

"Because if any thugs are on the lookout for you and Heaven, they'll probably be looking for you sitting together in the front seat. With Heaven back here, we're not so much of a target."

Or . . . not.

Teddy laughed. "Yeah. Whatever. That's the stupidest reason I've ever heard. Listen, we're gonna get married, so she should sit up front." He stomped off to the booth to pay.

Shit.

Hiro turned to me as soon as Teddy was out of earshot. "What did he say?" he said in a low voice. "Married?" He looked extremely angry, then hurt.

"It's not like that!" I said. "I told Teddy I'd marry him so that we could drive somewhere else and so that I could escape! It was a way to placate him . . . You don't understand . . . I ran into Teddy at a nightclub in Vegas, then Katie and I were attacked, then Teddy saved us, then we split, going to Joshua Tree, and—"

"Shhh, he's coming back," Hiro whispered.

"Seriously," I pleaded. "It didn't mean anything!"

I had been wondering when Teddy would let the cat out of the bag. It had been only a matter of time, but I'd wanted to tell Hiro myself.

But *why* had I told Teddy I'd marry him in the first place?

I knew that it had been for a good reason – to provide an opportunity for my escape. But . . . now it seemed wrong.

Had I ruined everything?

Hiro opened the back door and got back in the car. I couldn't tell from his blank expression how he was feeling. I followed him. Teddy looked at me questioningly, but I shot a look back at him. I wanted him to understand. But what could I say? *Secretly, my promise to marry you was all a sham? I'm in love with this other guy who's in the backseat? But I don't know exactly what he's feeling, and I want to find out? If I say the wrong thing, he might bolt?* I wanted Teddy to understand, to accept it. But I didn't think that was going to be very easy. Basically, Teddy was in the same position with me as I was with Hiro. A delicate balancing act. It must have been heartbreaking for him.

Teddy gunned the engine, and I looked searchingly at Hiro. "So, you found Katie, huh?" Hiro asked quietly, picking up on the information I'd just given him before Teddy came back from paying for gas.

"I did," I said. "It wasn't so hard, really. But I was only with her for a day. And then I found—"

"What are you two talking about back there?" Teddy asked loudly.

"Vegas," Hiro said.

"Oh, Vegas. That town sucks," Teddy answered. "Everyone's so uppity up in that place. Never let a man get the job done. Never let a guy relax!"

"Gambling debts," I whispered to Hiro. He nodded.

"More ninjas were there, right?" Hiro asked.

"Two attacks," I said. I wasn't planning on making mention of the fact that during the first run-in with the ninjas, I'd been really drunk. I hoped Teddy wouldn't mention it, either. "Teddy got me out of the first round."

Teddy found a techno station and turned the volume up. "Now we've got some tunes!" he said.

"I thought you only liked gangsta rap," I said.

"Nah, I like this shit, too," Teddy said. He started to wag his head to the beat.

Then the song began to play. "Heaven's Gone". The garbled Japanese lyrics floated out through looped tracks. Heavy drums came in. The voice rose and fell. *All the boys they ask, Where's Heaven at?*

I winced.

And Konishi, he not my boy, he got her locked in a tower . . .

"Konishi? Heaven?" Hiro said.

"Yo, Heaven, it's your song," Teddy said, tapping the steering wheel to provide a beat. Outside, the arid landscape flashed by. I wondered how long it would take to get to the border.

"Is this really your song?" Hiro asked. "What is this?"

"Um, I don't know," I said, searching for a way to change the subject.

"When Heaven and I get married, I'm pullin' this from

the airwaves," Teddy said. "You'd better believe it. Listen to what they're making up."

"Is this played everywhere?" Hiro said. His face had gone pale. He looked downright shocked. Hiro wasn't a big radio listener or club-goer. He obviously hadn't heard of Funkitout yet.

"I think it's more of a club song," I explained. "And usually everyone at clubs is dancing or drinking or on drugs or something, so they don't hear the words."

"How many times have you heard it?" Hiro asked.

"A couple of times. Just at clubs, though," I said. Hiro looked extremely worried.

"I thought you said you'd never heard it," Teddy said. I flinched. "Well, anyway, even though I'm totally pullin' it once we marry, this is like an underground smash!" he said. "Everyone loves you!"

"This isn't good," Hiro said. He seriously looked like he was freaking out, maybe wondering what in the world he was doing in this car with us.

"Hey, man, if you're so worried, I can leave you off somewhere," Teddy said. "You don't have to take the plunge into Mexico with us."

"It's not that," Hiro said. "I just don't like the idea of Heaven's name being broadcast all over the airwaves, even if it is just in clubs. What if the song gets bigger?"

"That's why I'm pulling it when we get married," Teddy said.

"Teddy, will you stop saying that?" I said, annoyed.

Teddy sniffed in the front seat. He opened his mouth to say something, then shut it. He paused for a minute, cranking the song louder.

She looks good, she licks good, she's tied up in a box . . .

I blushed.

"Are they just making all this up?" Hiro asked.

"Of course," I said. "Don't be ridiculous. When have I ever been tied up in a box?"

"Yo, that'd be *phat*!" Teddy said from the front.

"Hey!" I said. I saw Hiro's fists ball up.

"I'm kidding, man," Teddy said. "You know, a *joke*?" He winked at me in the rearview mirror.

This time Hiro sniffed.

"You can leave, you know," Teddy repeated, seeing Hiro's uncomfortable expression in the mirror.

Hiro didn't answer. Teddy drove on, obviously annoyed. Hiro looked out the window. I could see relief flood his face when the song ended and the DJ didn't mention the name of the last track.

We stopped for some coffee and ice cream. Teddy said he'd wait in the car. "Just get me a tall cappuccino or some shit like that," he said.

Walking away from the car, Hiro took my arm. He made a guttural, grumbling sort of noise. "I don't like that we're with him," he said. He turned back to me. "But I *am* glad I found you."

My heart melted.

"In that bus station . . . and . . . and you running into that burning house, God . . . ," he started. He opened his mouth to say something further, but nothing came out.

We grabbed the food and headed back out. I wanted to take Hiro's hand but was too uncertain of what he'd do. As soon as we came out through the rest stop's double doors, Teddy laid on the horn. "Yo, peeps!" Teddy bellowed. "You comin' or not?"

We climbed back into the car. Teddy's face was bright red. The car was full of smoke.

"God, Teddy, what's the *deal*?" I said, gagging on the earthy smell. "You have *drugs* on you? You were going to bring *drugs* over the border?"

"Naw, I had like a pinch. Hardly anything. And nothin' else," Teddy said. "I figured I'd better use it up before we hit Mexico." His eyes were red.

"Are you all right to drive?" Hiro asked.

"Yo, you think I would do anything that would endanger Heaven?"

I looked at Hiro and shrugged. What could we do? It turned out Teddy was an okay driver. He wasn't high. He was just supermoody. About a mile past the rest stop he angrily turned back at us and glared at Hiro. "Answer me one thing," he said. "*Why* are you coming along again?"

"Because," I answered. I tried not to sound angry, but I was getting pretty fed up.

Teddy angrily spun the dial and found a rap station.

"My boy, 50 Cent!" he said, and started bobbing his head to the music.

I sighed in relief. I was scared that Teddy was going to start a fight while he was driving. I looked at Hiro. He smiled in a clandestine sort of way. "Hey," he said softly. My insides turned over. I had to brush against him to get settled on my side. His skin was soft, warm. I felt my cheeks flushing.

Teddy had the radio volume turned up to almost maximum, probably out of annoyance. Maybe so he could get "all focused". But there were no back speakers, so Hiro and I realized we could talk without Teddy hearing. We started out slow, commenting on what was happening on the ride so far. It was weird – there was no tension or awkwardness in the air. It was like old times again, before Karen. Only better. Something else was there.

I wasn't sure how far to go when asking about Karen. "So how did she take it when you left?" I asked.

"Not so well, of course," Hiro said. "I told her it was something I had to do. We ended up having a pretty rational conversation the next day after our argument . . ." He trailed off. I could tell he was upset over whatever had happened. "She just . . . she wasn't honest with me. She wasn't the person I thought she was. She has no strength. I don't know if this makes any sense. She's a wonderful person, but . . . she needs something else. She doesn't need me."

"So . . . it's over?" I asked. I needed to hear it from his mouth. His sexy, pink, kissable mouth.

"It is," he said. "I wouldn't be here, giving up what I had in L.A., if it weren't."

I shivered.

"But that's what I don't understand," I said, thinking about this in my head. "I've been turning this over and over in my mind this whole car ride. The mission you gave me was to forget you. Yet I called, and here you are. And you seem . . . you seem okay that I've failed the mission. How does that work?"

Hiro laughed. He was so cute when he laughed – his eyes crinkled up, his hands sort of fluttered; I could see his beautiful, even white teeth when he smiled. "I wasn't sure how you'd interpret the mission I gave you. I knew that it was a risk. But the fact that you called me, even though I ordered you to forget me, proves your loyalty to your sensei," he explained. "That was your mission: to test your loyalty. It wasn't to forget me. That was the ploy."

"What?" I said.

"You had to understand it for yourself, you see," he said.

"But . . . I was losing my mind not calling you," I said. "For reasons other than . . ." I trailed off. I couldn't quite admit my feelings to Hiro yet. It was still a gamble. I still couldn't quite tell if Hiro was looking out for me in a brotherly, loving sort of way or if he actually had real feelings for me. I mean, it *seemed* like he was behaving differently, or was I just romanticizing the situation? I couldn't tell.

"Your calling me proves that you didn't just run off and forget everything you've learned from me as your sensei," Hiro said. "And . . . maybe other things, too." He blushed.

"Other things?" I said. My heart started to race. Okay, maybe I wasn't losing my mind.

"Other things . . . ," Hiro said. He put his hand over mine. He opened his mouth, but no sound came out. "Heaven, there are things . . . I want to tell you . . . I feel . . ."

I blinked. "Yes?" I said, the words coming out in barely more than a whisper.

"I . . . I'm just happy you called," he said finally. He squeezed my hand. The air around us grew hot. I knew something was different because Hiro wasn't explaining my mission by using any sort of parable or metaphor. To prove my loyalty was something Hiro had needed me to do – not really for my training at all. But to show him how I felt.

I shivered inside. Could that really be it?

Even the techno song on the radio seemed romantic. My heart pounded. I took a quick glance at Teddy. He was fuming up there, glancing at us in the rearview mirror. He saw Hiro's hand over mine.

"I'm glad I called, too," I whispered. We looked at each other and smiled.

Teddy sighed loudly, glancing back at us. He lowered the volume of the radio. So ended our conversation. But we kept holding hands, off and on, the rest of the way to Mexico.

Teddy glared at me from the front seat. "We're almost at the border," he said. His eyes weren't red anymore. "We need to come up with a plan."

"I thought you said you knew someone," I said.

"I do, but I don't know how he's going to deal with *three* of us. Two, maybe, but not three." He eyed me.

"How do you know this guy?" I asked suspiciously.

"Used to come down here with, you know, little drugs. Guy never searched me. Always got a kickback. But . . ."

"So are you sure this guy is working?" I asked.

"I called him before we left. He'll be there. But as I was saying, I don't know . . . maybe two instead of three . . . Honestly, the best thing to do is for you to hide."

"What, me?" I asked, still drowsy. "Where?"

"Well . . . maybe the trunk."

Hiro looked at him. "I don't like this trunk idea," he said.

"Dude, I don't either, but—"

"I'll go in the trunk," Hiro said quickly. "I don't want Heaven in there."

"Hiro . . . ," I started. "That doesn't make any sense. No one is looking for you. But people *are* looking for me. And possibly for Teddy, too." I shot him a sidelong glance. Teddy nodded. I swallowed quickly. "I guess I'll go in the trunk."

"No way," Hiro said. "I'm going. Pull over."

Teddy pulled the car over to the side of the road. Hiro got out and stood impatiently at the back of the car.

"Couldn't we at least *try* to get past this guy at the gate with three of us?" I asked Teddy angrily.

"Heaven . . . ," Teddy said, looking at me intently. I could see a great amount of desire in his eyes – and loss. "What's up with you two? Are you, like, in love or something? This has been the weirdest drive of my life . . . the weirdest couple of days of my life . . . and, well, you know how I feel . . ."

I sighed. I'd wondered when he was going to ask this question. "I don't know what's going on," I said. "I'm sorry. I . . . I can't explain it. I mean, maybe nothing, but . . . Hiro has helped me. There's something . . ." I wasn't making any sense. But in Teddy's eyes, I could see a certain understanding. He nodded in an almost heartfelt way.

"All right," he said. "I get it." He sounded so utterly sad. "I see how it is."

"But . . . ," I said. I didn't know what I was trying to say. I knew I couldn't placate Teddy by lying, by making something up. I had to tell him the truth. We were friends. "I'm sorry," I said quietly.

"No biggie," Teddy said. It seemed like he'd just brushed off his feelings. He stared out at the cars passing on the highway. I sensed Teddy was fighting back the urge to say something else, something that hurt too much. He then quickly shot out of the front seat and went to confer with Hiro, who was still standing expectantly at the back of the car.

We drove to the border. I saw the large border police structures rising in the distance and my heart started to race. We were seriously going to Mexico. Hiro calmly stared straight ahead. He must have sensed I was getting nervous because he turned to me, put his hand over mine, and smiled. Through the nerves, I got a rush of lust. I had to realize and re-realize, with every minute, that Hiro was here. It hadn't sunk in yet at all.

Teddy pulled to the border and found his friend at the gate. They exchanged a few words in Spanish, and we were allowed to pass. Our passports weren't even scrutinized. We drove on through the Mexican landscape, as arid and yellow as Arizona, yet something felt different, foreign. I was out of the United States.

"Pablo wants to give out the passports in the hotel," Teddy said. "He suggested we get a room since they might not be ready once we get there. Although I'm not stayin' in the dirtbag place that he's in. We'll stay at this place around the street. You guys got cash to pay for it?"

"I do," Hiro said.

Teddy looked at him, as if he was surprised that Hiro had cash on him. "Can you cover the cost of a room in a fleabag hotel, compadre?" he said, eyeing Hiro in the rearview mirror. Hiro nodded.

"Okay, then," Teddy said. "We'll pick up the passports,

go back to our room to arrange the flight, then get some sleep and hopefully head out in the morning."

We pulled up to the hotel that Pablo was supposed to be in. Hiro quickly checked in, saying that he was alone, to prevent any suspicion. (Although I really wondered – who would be looking for us in Tijuana? It seemed a little unlikely, but I guessed it was good to take the precaution.) Soon Hiro came back to us with a key swinging from his finger. We opened the door to the slightly sordid looking room. Hiro threw down his backpack and sat on the bed.

"Don't get too comfortable," Teddy said. "We gotta go do what we came for."

"Teddy, can you go on your own?" I said. "All I want to do right now is sleep."

Teddy looked at me angrily. "What, you're not going to come?" he said. "Heaven, I'm doing this in part for you. The least you can do is come with me."

I stared at him. I desperately needed to be alone with Hiro. Although I'd been trying to be very patient with Teddy, I was starting to lose it a little. I needed him to just leave us be, if even for an hour or so. If it was just Hiro and me, I doubted we'd be in this situation right now. Why were we in Mexico? In Tijuana? Did I really *want* to go to Switzerland? Why was Teddy calling the shots? I must have given him an incredible look of annoyance and desperation because he finally threw his hands up. "I'm sick of you people," he said. "As soon as we get these passports, we're going our separate ways. In fact, I may get my own room tonight."

"We have to stick together, remember?" I reminded him.

Teddy glared at me. "Remind me why?" he snarled. Then he slammed the door.

I looked at Hiro and smiled. "He'll be back," I said. I lay down on the bed. Finally we were alone.

Heaven in that little voice she's got, saying, "Oh, I don't know what it is, I can't explain it," and then lover boy over there's gazing at her as if she's the first chick he's ever laid eyes on in his life, and . . . ugh, it was nasty. A nasty car ride. She didn't want to get married. She never did. It was all . . . I don't know what it was. She was holding out for that dolt. That straight, square white boy of a Japanese kid if I ever saw one. What was with the little sniff when I mentioned drugs? Brother, I'm getting you this far into TJ, you better show me some respect! And what's worse, I hate Mexico. The bugs, the cockroaches . . . I guess I have two options once I get these passports for everyone. One: I go alone and try to forget the bitch, which means I lose any money I had comin' to me. Or two: I try to get her back. Which would mean . . . what? Killing Hiro? Getting someone else to kill him? That bastard . . . He helped her fight off my dad's peeps in that whole kidnapping fiasco. And he's the one she's interested in.

Maybe I could get someone to do it for me. Make it look like an accident or something. And shit, am I really going to have to go through this ridiculous "kidnapping" thing with Pablo? What is that gonna require? Will Pablo just give me my passport and then we'll "pretend" that I've been kidnapped? Is my dad gonna buy that when secretly I'll be living it up near Lake Geneva with all the Swiss misses or maybe in Amsterdam, where they're never lacking for any kind of candy to amuse me for a night?

Dude, my father's not going to go for this.

I walk into the hotel lobby where Pablo's staying and glimpse myself in the dirty little mirror they've got behind the desk. I'm a billion times more fly than that Hiro jerk. He's a skinny kid with chicken arms and legs. He could wear chicks' clothes. And he always looks so damn serious. What the hell does she see in him? Is he loaded? I press the elevator button and ride up with this little honey in a short orange dress. She gives me the eyes, but I still feel miserable. This honey thinks I'm hot. Why doesn't Heaven?

I knock on the door to Pablo's. Why did he want me to meet him in a hotel room? Why not just a car? That meant we had to get a hotel room in this rattrap instead of just waiting it out in a café or whatever. (What are Heaven and Hiro doing while I'm gone? Having sex? What?) It takes Pablo forever to open the door. But when he does . . .

When he does, there's the barrel of a gun looking straight at me.

"Yo," I say under my breath.

Pablo's breath is putrid and his horrible rotting teeth spread into a smile. "Hola," he snarls. "Have a nice trip?"

I quiver and try and take this all in stride – sometimes the boy does this, just to mess with you. "Not bad," I say. "Considering." I duck my head a little.

Big mistake.

Pablo somehow manages to spin me into the hall and presses the gun into my back. "Now, do me a big favour," he says, pressing the gun into my spine even harder, "and take me to that little piece of Heaven you've got stashed in your room."

1 3

I waited until I heard the elevator ding on our floor. It slid closed. I peeked out the little hole in the door. Teddy was gone. I turned around. Hiro looked at me passionately. I started to shake – this was almost too much to handle.

Before I realized what was happening, Hiro ran up to me, grabbed my shoulders, and touched his lips to mine.

Wow.

I didn't know whether I should keep my eyes open or closed. His touch was so soft – he moved his hands from my shoulders to my face. Then to my hair. I waved my hands around for a moment, unsure what to do, then secured them tightly behind his back. I pulled him closer.

I felt like Amaterasu Omikami, the goddess who shines in the heavens. I felt like I was shining sun down onto my mortal self, smiling, spreading great golden light down onto my shoulders. Hiro wasn't clumsy when he kissed me, and he smelled wonderful – like this fantastic blend of apricots and spiciness – even though we'd been sitting in that rank car for hours. I was sure he could hear my heart pounding through my clothes. He held my face in his hands and gazed at me for a moment, out of breath.

"I'm sorry," he said. "I just had to do that." He stood back. "God, I'm so sorry . . ."

"No!" I said. "I mean, don't stop."

He stood back again. "Heaven, this is so important. What I feel for you is so strong. I've felt it always. Ever since I met you. I think I had a dream before I met you, a kind of premonition that you were coming." He smiled. "Look at me, I'm shaking. I'm so nervous to tell you all this . . ."

I held my breath. All the times I'd dreamed of Hiro – not before I met him, mind you – but all the times *recently* I'd dreamed of him. I'd thought this was one-sided! How in my wildest dreams was this becoming a reality?

"The last week has been so hard," he spluttered. "Really, the last couple of weeks. When I realized, it wasn't so long ago. But I was making something work that wasn't working. I just felt that something was wrong. I'm sorry that I didn't realize it sooner . . ."

I thought back to Hiro cuddling on the couch with Karen. Them kissing. Calling Hiro in the morning, Karen answering. What if this was as fleeting as that? What if Hiro changed his mind?

He waved his hand in the air, detecting something in my expression. "What I had with Karen was never meant to be. I sensed it from the *beginning*. But I thought, Maybe I'm wrong. I did care about her, and I thought over time it would become stronger. But now I know." He smiled slightly. "Now I know that I must trust my instincts. My instincts were telling me that I should be with you."

I sat down on the bed, overwhelmed. Hiro sat, too, and kissed me again. "I feel so strange telling you these things," he said. "I've never just admitted any of it and laid myself out like this. I feel so vulnerable, especially since I don't really know any of your feelings."

"You shouldn't worry," I said. "Haven't you *noticed*? I've had feelings for you since . . . since I don't even know when. Maybe when we met. I don't know. Soon after, anyway. When you got together with Karen, my heart was broken. I felt distanced. And when you told me . . . when I got on that bus to come to Vegas . . . it was like something died . . ."

Hiro looked a little stunned. "Are you serious?" he said.

"Yeah," I answered.

We didn't say anything for a few moments. We just stared at each other.

"I felt awful sending you to Vegas," Hiro said quietly. "I was the one who let you go! I realized my feelings for sure when you got on that bus. I thought, What if I've made a huge mistake? What if she gets herself killed?"

I thought about the ninjas. It had been very close. I
could have been killed.

And Teddy had saved me.

I brushed away my guilt about Teddy for the moment.
"But I didn't," I said to Hiro. "I'm here."

"Yes, you are," Hiro said. He kissed me again. God, it
was so wonderful. Kissing Hiro was better than any dream
I'd had about kissing him.

We kissed for nearly twenty minutes more, fumbling
around on the bed. Hiro took things slow. I obviously
couldn't think too much beyond that, sexually. Besides,
kissing felt too wonderful at the time. Occasionally Hiro
would move back for a moment and stare into my eyes. I
had never imagined that I'd be this close to him and that
he'd look at me this way. All of the tension between us that
had even lingered slightly in the car had shattered. If only
this moment could be extended forever. If only we didn't
have to worry about anything else.

And then, inexplicably, I started to cry.

Huge tears rolled down my cheeks. I couldn't get any
words out. I was choked. And mortified. I sat up, groping for
a tissue. Hiro looked at me while I exploded into more sobs.

"What is it?" he asked. "Oh my God. Have I done something wrong?"

"No," I answered, shaking my head. "You've done
something right. Honestly."

Hiro didn't say anything.

I continued, dabbing my eyes with a tissue. But as soon as I started talking, I began to cry again. I was overcome with emotion. Sadness, even. "It's just a release," I explained. "At this moment I suddenly feel . . . complete. And safe. Completely safe." I smiled, then sniffed. "Even though we're in Mexico, running for our lives. As you very well know, and as I really don't need to explain . . . I've felt so lost lately. I've had so many things taken from me."

"Yes," Hiro said, putting his hand over mine.

"My brother . . . ," I said, bursting into tears again. "He's gone . . ."

"I know," Hiro said, stroking my arm. "Come on."

"And my father . . . ," I said. My lip trembled.

"You've dealt with a lot," Hiro said.

"I just . . . I've felt like such a mess," I said. "Nothing has been going right. I went from completely sheltered to . . . to being attacked, like, every day! And . . . and then it was like everyone I was around . . . was just . . . awful things were happening to all of them . . . and Cheryl, is she alive? Does anyone know?"

Hiro shook his head. "I haven't heard anything," he said. "But then, I've stayed away from there."

I thought about Cheryl being consumed by the flames. She had helped me. A lump formed in my throat. "And . . . this is the only thing that's actually felt good for me. This is the only thing that's worked out in . . . forever. I was at the point where I just thought nothing would work for me ever again. And I was at the point where I thought I'd never see you ever again."

My eyes welled up with tears all over again. Hiro held my hands. "I wouldn't have let that happen," he said.

"But you almost did!" I blurted. "You put me on a bus to Vegas! How could you just . . . leave me . . . if you had these feelings?"

Hiro hung his head. "I know," he admitted. "I went too far. I realize that now . . . It was completely idiotic that I let you go out to Vegas. I knew full well the yakuza connections there." Now his face crumpled up as if *he* was about to cry. I put my hand on his arm.

"But that's the amazing thing," he said. "You are fine. You are a survivor. This is why I'm so crazy about you, Heaven. You're so strong. You don't even realize it, but . . . you're so special."

My insides shimmered. I wiped my eyes. I didn't quite feel so emotional anymore. Or rather, I felt a good sort of emotion. I felt completely in love.

"I'm glad you rode up on that motorcycle when you did," I said, laughing.

"So what about Teddy?" Hiro asked.

I related the story of finding Katie, hitting a dance club (omitting the drinking part of the evening, as well as the part with the boys), going to the bathroom, and running smack into Teddy. "It was bizarre," I said. "I didn't know if I should trust him or not, but then I thought, He helped us with the kidnapping . . ."

"I didn't know you were going to be with Teddy when I came to Joshua Tree. I thought maybe you were with Katie."

"You didn't think I was with Teddy?" I said. "But I think I said that in the message!"

Hiro looked at me sadly. "I didn't *get* the message," he said. "And Karen didn't explain that part."

Oh. Right. *Duh.*

I continued to explain the Teddy story, getting to the part where I agreed to marry him. "I needed us to get out of there. I needed to move to somewhere where I could escape and actually get away. Get on a bus, a train, whatever. At Joshua Tree, there was nothing for miles. I couldn't have run forever." I looked down at my hands. "I feel a little bad that I agreed, in all truth. Teddy was so excited. And it wasn't for the money. He was excited because I think he was actually . . . interested in me."

"Well, that was pretty obvious from the way he behaved during the car ride. I felt a little strange barging in like that, but I couldn't let you go a second time."

"Believe me, you weren't barging in," I said, laughing.

"But why didn't you wait for me?" Hiro asked.

"I didn't know," I said. "Remember? What did I know at that point? And you hadn't got the message. I thought you were through with me . . ."

Hiro let out a long, laboured sigh, then wrapped his

arms around me. "Never again," he said. "I'm here now. Your great protector."

"At last," I said, snuggling into his arms. Even though Hiro was wiry and muscular, there was a softness about him. A warmth. I sighed happily.

Hiro backed away for a moment. I looked up. "What?" I said.

"Nothing," he said quickly, trying to hug me again.

I sensed he wanted to say something. "No, what?"

He cleared his throat. "Well, I'm just wondering. It's not possible that you're interested in me because . . . well . . . because I was sort of this . . . person who watched over you and protected you, is it?"

I thought about this hard. Why was it that I was interested in Hiro? I thought of his body, moving quickly and deftly as we went through our practices. I thought of his laugh whenever I'd say something funny. I thought about that time I'd walked in on him sleeping: the gentle way he'd hugged the pillow, his mouth hanging open, his hair standing up straight. And although at first perhaps that was why I'd hung on to Hiro, I realized now that Hiro-as-protector was not what I wanted in my life. I'd struck out on my own, first to Cheryl's, then to Vegas. And I was still alive. I'd even made it through a few days with Teddy without losing my mind or succumbing to some Yukemura marriage plot. I was a survivor on my own.

No. I wanted Hiro as a boyfriend.

I smiled. "Not at all," I said. I explained to him the thoughts that had just gone through my head. Hiro nodded happily, hugging me tight. "I'm so happy," he said.

"You said it." I sighed. We began to kiss again.

But this time, midkiss, a horrible splintering noise broke the air. We shot apart just in time to see the door to our room broken open with what looked like a hatchet. My whole body tensed up. Hiro tensed up, too.

Before we could do anything, a huge guy with a slimy mustache burst into the room. He wore a dirty white shirt and jeans and steel-toed shoes. There must have been about six guys behind him. He stared at Hiro and me. He licked his lips.

"Well, look at this," he said. I shuddered and sprang off the bed, backing into a corner. Hiro followed me.

"Is this Miss Heaven . . . Kogo?" He had enormous gold chains around his neck and extremely brown teeth.

I didn't answer.

"Okay, baby, you just stay real still," he said. He pulled out a long knife and waved it at me. It looked like there was crusted blood on the tip. The guys behind him pulled out various weapons and brandished them in the air. "And who is your little friend?"

The crowd parted a little. More guys moved in. The ring-leader guy moved closer. And then, cutting through the line of men, in walked Pablo, the guy from the VIP room in Vegas. He looked a little grimier now, but his hair was still slicked back and shiny and he still wore about a thousand rings.

He stood in front of the steel-tipped-boots guy. "So, we meet again," he said. He looked me up and down in a perverse way. "But you're cheating on your husband-to-be, aren't you?"

"Wha?" I said.

"No matter," Pablo said, not letting me finish. The group started to move again, pushing someone to the front. Teddy. His eye had swollen shut and he was bound at the wrists.

"Oh my God," I breathed in. The air stood still for a moment.

Then Teddy's good eye met mine. He looked at me with utter desperation and mouthed, "I'm sorry."

1 4

Hiro sprang for the ringleader guy, wresting the knife out of his hands. I shoved Teddy down and lunged at Pablo, kicking him first on the shoulder, then in the stomach. He flailed back but recovered quickly.

"A little fireball!" he said, sneering, and then pulled out a gun.

I quickly knocked it out of his hand and lunged at him again. He blocked me with his body and I realized, *These guys can't really fight*. I barraged him with a series of roundhouse kicks and jabs to his jaw. He recoiled in pain and swung blindly at me. Another guy behind him grabbed him and shoved him back.

"You're in trouble," the new guy said. He had about three teeth and extremely long, stringy hair. And gigantic biceps.

There was no way I could flip him, so I concentrated on moving quickly to elude him. He swung, but I dodged out of his way. I quickly checked on Hiro – he was still battling the leader guy. On the floor Teddy scurried to the corner, trying to wriggle out of his restraints.

Three Teeth swung at me again, this time making contact. The side of my head stung with white pain and I stepped back. I saw through blurred vision that Hiro stepped in and managed to trip the thug. He came careening towards me. I shouted and scrambled out of his way, cracking my already hurt head on a bedpost. I bent over in pain. For a split second, with my eyes closed, I could only hear the grunts and cracks of Hiro fighting all these guys at once.

I quickly regained my wits and went to work on some of the other guys again. Three Teeth looked like he was down for the count, and Pablo was nowhere to be seen. Another Mexican in a turquoise T-shirt ran towards me with his fists flying. I managed to block the punches but this time cracked my hip on the edge of the bureau.

"Ahhh!" I wailed in pain. If the banditos didn't kill me, fighting in this damn hotel room would. Turquoise T-shirt stood back, laughing at me. So I gave him an ul gul chi reu gi – a tae kwon do punch to the face. He howled and staggered back.

Hiro was doing okay. He'd managed to get a couple of the thugs to the ground and was collecting their guns. But then another wave of them entered the room. The place was nearly filled to capacity. And it was all of them versus . . . three of us.

Where the hell were the hotel managers? Did this sort of thing happen all the time?

Teddy hovered near the window and finally managed to get his hands free. He started to throw anything that wasn't bolted down at the assailants. A phone book flew through the air. The phone came next. Shoes. Anything. I ducked out of their way as they came flying through the air. Hiro swung his legs around to trip up one of the men, quickly grabbing his knife. Someone crept up behind him, though, and snatched the purloined gun that he had lodged in the back of his jeans. The man pointed the gun at his head. I shouted. But then Hiro spun around and knocked it out of his hand again. I let my breath out and concentrated on who was in front of me – a guy who'd lost his weapon somewhere in the skirmish and was now brandishing a table lamp. He lifted it over his head – it looked like it was ceramic and heavy. He tossed it at me, but I ducked. The lamp sailed across the room and flew right into Teddy, breaking into a million pieces on impact.

It knocked him out cold.

Shards of it flew everywhere. I covered my eyes. I was afraid that the banditos would try to hurt Teddy – shoot him or something – while he was unconscious, so I took on about six of them, trying to take them on all at once. I started with a series of roundhouse kicks, flailing my arms and my legs, basically just blindly fighting. I managed to look over at Hiro and saw that he was doing the same thing – taking on too many guys, not doing too well in the process. I cracked one guy upside the head, and when he fell, I looked over just in time to see one of the banditos swipe Hiro's legs with his knife. Hiro howled in pain.

"Noooo!" I said.

My palms were slick with blood. I didn't know if it was my own or someone else's. I tried to move the men away from Teddy, who was still unconscious behind the bed, but suddenly there was Pablo, back in the room, waving a gun around.

"Enough!" he cried. He held up his hands in halt. He pointed the gun at me.

Hiro and I froze. Was he going to shoot us? If we tried to knock his gun away, the others might draw out their guns. I didn't know what to do. The guns Hiro and I had knocked out of their hands were scattered around the room. I couldn't see any at the moment.

I quickly looked over to Teddy and saw that his eyes were open. He was staring at the banditos and their guns with a look of utter terror. The kingpin of the operation, Pablo – the guy who'd screamed "enough" – was very close to Teddy's leg. He could grab the gun from him and gain an advantage.

"Go," I mouthed ever so slightly to Teddy. "Grab him."

192

Teddy nodded and started to feebly move over. *Faster*! I thought. Teddy moved very, very slowly. But then he looked up at me. His eyes looked dead. He closed them, and to my horror, he started to move *away* from the guy with the gun. He slumped back down and closed his eyes.

He's pretending! I thought. *He's playing dead! What a coward!* Before I knew what I was doing, I lunged across the bed and knocked the gun from the bandito's hand. It flew into the air almost in slow motion and landed somewhere on the ground. And then it fired.

A smattering of sparks filled the room. I squeezed my eyes shut and covered my head, hoping the bullet wasn't aimed in my direction. After the shot had been fired, I didn't feel any pain. I didn't think it got me. But where had the bullet gone? I opened my eyes and prayed that Hiro hadn't been hit, either. But I could see that he wasn't. He was looking around, just as confused as I was.

Then I saw. Teddy. He wasn't moving. I could see a hole at the back of his shirt.

Had the bullet got him? "Teddy?" I yelled.

He didn't respond.

"Oh my God," I said. I began to feel woozy. Had it really got him? Despite my distaste for blood and death, I had to see . . .

I took a step forward but felt something cold at my back. I didn't turn around, but I just knew it was one of the banditos. He had me in a hold that I couldn't get out of. I couldn't flip him. I let out a weak cry, then glanced over at Hiro. He was being held, too. We were both powerless.

"There's nothing you can do about him now," said a voice in broken English. "So we're going to take a little ride."

They bound our arms behind our backs. I cursed and coughed and wrenched my head to see Teddy. Hiro struggled and broke free and started to swipe at the banditos. The banditos whipped after him. I kicked my legs. The guy who was holding me whacked them with something that resembled a billy club.

Hiro yelped from around the corner. They dragged him back into the doorway, slapping his face, punching him in the stomach. I gasped. I'd never seen Hiro beaten this badly. "No!" I cried weakly.

They finally stopped and managed to tie up Hiro's hands again. They started to herd us into the hall. I twisted around to see Teddy. If he was still lying there. If he was breathing. Anything.

But to my surprise, he was gone.

"Hiro," I whispered as the banditos shoved us out the door. "Teddy's gone!"

"No talking!" someone barked. It sounded like Pablo.

"What?" Hiro said, out of breath. His nose was bleeding.

I twisted my neck around to see the corner where Teddy had been lying. Above him was an open window. He must have escaped.

But wait. We were on the fourth floor. Could he have dropped down that far?

They shoved us down the back stairs, through murky-smelling alleys. I cascaded against the slimy walls and felt bruises immediately rise to the surface of my skin. Unfortunately, we didn't end up at the front of the hotel, so I wasn't able to see if Teddy was lying in a pool of blood on the concrete. But I was sure that between the bullet and the fall, he was dead. The banditos shoved us roughly to a back alley.

We reached a large black sedan. Three guys had appeared from nowhere and grabbed me from the other guy and wrenched my arms behind my back and tied them together. Then they shoved me in the car. My legs, covered in blood, stuck to the leather. Hiro was in the backseat, too. I was too terrified to even feel relief. Hiro was a mess, too – his face was bloody and his legs looked terrible. I stared at him in terror and confusion. He stared back.

Pablo rolled into the front seat and glared at us. "I told you not to talk," he said, even though we hadn't said anything. "If you talk, I'll slowly cut off various parts of your body. First your ears, maybe. Then perhaps your arms. Then maybe your lips. You have beautiful lips, you know?"

He held up a long, terrible-looking knife, which made me think he wasn't kidding.

Pablo eyed Hiro. "You been kissing those lips, boy?" Hiro didn't say a word. The blood from his nose had dripped to his chin and onto his shirt.

Pablo lit a cigarette. The guy in the steel-toed shoes rolled into the passenger seat; I could see his weaselly face in the rearview mirror. Finally the car squealed into life and jerked into movement. The cigarette smoke began to fill the car – I suddenly realized it was a cigar, heavy and stinking. I nearly gagged. My body felt a new kind of pain from the brawl we'd just finished.

I kept hoping Teddy would emerge with his gun and blow these guys to bits. He *had* to. He'd always escaped before.

The car rolled out of the parking lot. Where were we going? My heart pounded. Teddy must have died while trying to get out of the window. How had he done it without us noticing? But then, it *had been* loud in there with those guys just trying to contain Hiro and me.

We rolled out of sight.

No one was coming to rescue us.

Pablo said something to the other guy in Spanish. They laughed, then Pablo lit a new cigar. They glared at us in the rearview mirror. I opened and closed my fists, trying to figure out what to do. I tried to look to Hiro for strength, but he didn't look very brave right then. He looked as terrified as I was.

Coming soon

samurai girl The Book of the Flame

I am home. Back with the family and life that I once knew and longed for.

But something here isn't right. Can I really trust my family?

I must know my enemy.

I am Samurai Girl.

Turn the page for the first chapter . . .

Tokyo
Daily
News

At 12:03 A.M. last night, per police logs, a burglary was reported by staff at the exclusive Kazashi Clinic in Mizuho. Go Watanebe, the clinic's director, declined comment, but an anonymous source told the *Daily News* that around 11 P.M., a nurse discovered that the clinic's drug supplies had been plundered. "They knew what they were doing," the source said, "because they took a bunch of morphine and Valium and other drugs with a high street-market value." Police refused to answer questions about a possible link between the drug theft and Konishi Kogo (currently the clinic's most well known patient), who was flown back to Japan two months ago after an attack by an unknown assailant in Los Angeles. Okichi Ono, head nurse at the clinic, stated that Kogo is in stable condition but remains comatose. Kogo's adopted daughter, Heaven Kogo, has been missing since her wedding day four months ago, when a masked intruder (some sources hsave said a ninja) disrupted the ceremony and murdered her borother, Ohiko Kogo.

Las Vegas Sun

February 28, 2004

Police are searching for a man who they believe may have information about Heaven Kogo, a Japanese national currently on the California State Police's missing persons list. The man was recently seen in several Strip locales, including the Hard Rock Hotel and Mandalay Bay, in the company of a woman fitting the description of Heaven Kogo. Sources describe the man as a "high roller" who frequents VIP rooms at casinos and clubs on the Strip and who sometimes travels with an entourage. Anyone with information about the above individual is asked to call 1-800-TIPS4US.

1

"Shut up. And tell your boyfriend to shut up, too," Pablo snapped.

I clamped my mouth shut and looked over at Hiro, who sat next to me in the backseat of the black sedan. An ugly-looking bruise was spreading across Hiro's left cheek (those beautiful cheekbones!) and blood trickled down his forehead. His lower lip was swollen, and his jeans were covered in dirt and more blood. And if the pain that racked my body was any sign, I didn't look much better myself. We'd just crossed the Mexican border into California (thanks to the handful of cash I'd seen Pablo cram into the customs officer's pocket), and I had no idea where we were headed.

Hiro shook his head at me slowly.

"Do what he says," he mouthed, and I nodded, trying to stop the swell of tears I felt stinging my eyes. It was unbearable to think that I might be leading Hiro to his death. This was my fight, my battle, and these thugs, whoever they were, wanted me, not him. Now, for the first time since my long journey had begun, I couldn't see a way out. We were going almost a hundred miles an hour through the California desert. My hands were tightly bound behind my back, with a rope connecting them to my ankles, which were also bound. I felt like a cow being led to the slaughter, helpless and doomed.

I was propped up awkwardly against Hiro, unable to sit up straight. After a few minutes I felt him writhing against me. "Are you hurt?" I whispered. Hiro shook his head but kept squirming. I looked nervously toward the front seat, where Pablo sat puffing a huge cigar and driving way too fast. It was hard to believe that when Teddy had introduced me to Pablo back in Vegas, I hadn't immediately sensed what a dangerous guy he was — as if the blingy jewelry and greased-back hair weren't enough, he had a mouthful of gold teeth. I prayed he and his cohort wouldn't turn around.

I glanced back at Hiro. The veins on his neck stuck out from the effort he was making not to move as he worked at the cord around his wrists. I held my breath right along with him, willing Pablo and Co. not to look. I wasn't sure if "escape artist" was on Hiro's list of abilities, but I hoped so.

Hiro gave a tight-lipped smile. I looked down. The ropes holding him had gone slack. He'd wriggled his way out.

My heart leapt. Maybe this wasn't the end. Hiro motioned with his eyes that I should maneuver into a position where he could work on the knots that bound me without being seen. I scooted around in the seat, focused all the time on Pablo and his buddy, who both seemed to be intent on celebrating with their nasty-smelling cigars. In between puffs they growled at each other in Spanish, and the unknown thug, who had a bristling mustache that couldn't hide the ugly scar slashing across his lip and down his jawline, kept gesturing with his gun for emphasis.

In a few moments I was free. I resisted the urge to stretch my arms and legs—or to hurl myself into Hiro's arms, to hug him and tell him I was sorry for this, for all of this. As if in answer to my thoughts, the car jolted without warning, throwing Hiro against me.

"Your mission is to achieve heightened perception," he whispered in my ear. "You must be aware of everything around you. That's the only way you're going to make it."

"What's going on back there? Didn't I tell you to shut up?" Mustache (as I'd come to think of him) turned around and waved his gun at us. My heart pounded as I cringed back against the seat. Having a gun shoved in your face in real life is freaking scary. Any bravery you might have on top just oozes right out of you. And I was terrified he'd notice that we were no longer tied up.

"I just wanted to make sure she was okay," Hiro said, his voice calm.

"You can't help your little girlfriend anymore," Mustache leered, his grin twisted and grotesque. "Just do as you're told."

He turned around, and Hiro gave me a look that said, "Simmer down." I stared out the window into the glaring heat.

I had a lot of work to do. First I had to pull myself out of my body to try to forget about the pain and stiffness that always set in after a fight. Then I had to clear my head of the images—the gang of mystery men bursting into our hotel room, the thud and thunk of the bone-crushing kicks and punches, the sight of Teddy sliding down to the ground, his back covered in blood. . . .